"iSSUES..."

By Robert Stevens Jr.

This is a work of fiction. All of the characters, organizations, and events portrayed in this novel are either products of the author's imagination or are used fictitiously. Any resemblance to actual persons, living or dead, events, or locals is extremely coincidental.

"iSSUES…" Copyright © 2011 by Robert Stevens, Jr.

All Rights Reserved

Edited by Kimberley T. Cross

For more information go to

www.rob-stevens-jr-author.com

www.stevensrobert67@gmail.com

ISBN-13: 978-1470016135

ISBN-10: 1470016133

Cover Art: "All is Vanity (1892)" By Charles A. Gilbert (September 3, 1873-Apriol 20, 1929)

CHAPTER ONE

2009: Dr. Monica "Reese" Withers, a 35 year old woman, lived in Cambridge and practiced psychiatry in Boston, Massachusetts. Monica envisioned being a psychiatrist since she was a little girl when her mother and father took her to see Dr. Thomas for an issue she could no longer recall. Reese cherished fond memories of Dr. Thomas who rewarded her with her favorite orange, yellow, and brown candies after each session and ended every session with a corny joke. And as you've probably inferred…Reese's nickname was derived from her childhood addiction to the candy Reese's Pieces.

Reese wasn't married nor did she have any kids; her career was ALWAYS her first priority. All of her friends were either married, in long term relationships, or at least dating a marriage prospect. Not a day passed that Reese's girlfriends didn't try to set her up with a one of their spouse's friends or some supercilious football player trying to recover the luster of his college days. Yet, Reese always contended that she'd have plenty of time for marriage and children after her reputation was firm in the community, and she expanded her practice to other counties or maybe open offices in lower class communities where people would have the same psychological help but at an affordable cost.

Today Reese arrived at her office located in the John Hancock building at 9 am like she did every Monday thru Friday. Reese shut the engine off and grabbed her things from the passenger side seat. As Reese opened the car door and proceeded to exit, someone grabbed the door and yanked her out of the car. "SAY ONE WORD BITCH AND I'LL END YOUR LIFE." The fairly stout man was wearing a ski mask protecting his identity. "Damn he is strong," Reese thought as she literally saw her life flash before her eyes. He had his hand over Reese's mouth while the other hand held a gun at Reese's stomach. "WHERE'S

THE FUCKING MONEY?" Reese slowly turned her head toward her purse which she had dropped in the seat. The man followed Reese's eyes to the purse and threatened, "ONCE AGAIN IF YOU MOVE OR TRY TO SCREAM I WILL PUT A BULLET IN YOUR GUT." Sweat poured down Reese's forehead as the man reached for her purse while nearly puncturing her abdomen with the gun. He snatched the purse and took a quick look inside; noticing the wallet and her cell phone inside, he thought, "This was a pretty good haul for the day." The man turned his attention back to Reese, "Damn you're purty..." he said in a strong Boston accent. "How 'bout you giving me some...hea?" Just then he heard voices coming from the bank of elevators. The voices echoed louder as they headed toward him and Reese. The man ascertained that he didn't have time to rape his victim nor would he have time to further batter her, so he looked at Reese and grinned. "Sorry Bitch maybe next time." Finally, he turned and ran for the stairwell. Reese began to feel dizzy, and she could no longer keep her balance; her knees became weak, and she collapsed on the hard concrete. Someone walking toward their car saw Reese and called 911.

The EMT's were taking care of Reese when the police arrived. Reese was sitting up on a stretcher with gauze covering the bump that she obtained from hitting the pavement. Officers Jim and John approached Reese to introduce themselves, but when the usually cool, suave Jim looked at Reese he was at such a loss for words that he couldn't finish his name. So John smirked at his partner then finished the introductions. While John questioned Reese about the incident, Jim couldn't stop evaluating Reese's beauty, despite her skewed appearance from the assault. Captain Jim Patrick Henry was a 25 year veteran with the Boston Police Department, and he was a tough, red-headed, sixth generation Irishmen from the mean streets of South Boston. His partner and best friend Lead

Detective John Campbell was a 30 year old transplant from Northern California.

Jim was determined to find the bastard that attacked Reese. So, Jim and John finished taking the necessary information and started their investigation of Reese's case. Given their tactics, Reese's case was solved in a matter of days, not weeks or months like most assault and robbery cases. Jim and John got a lead from a CI which led them straight to the perpetrator's whereabouts. Jim thirsted to bludgeon the criminal, yet he and John arrested the perpetrator without a reported incident to ensure the trial would result in a smooth conviction.

Jim, seeing his opportunity to get in good with Reese, went to her house in upscale Cambridge to tell her that the perpetrator was caught and arrested. Jim ejected with pride, "The perp plead guilty to the crime. So, the added bonus is that you don't have to testify." Grateful for

Jim's speedy detective work and breathtaking swagger, Reese invited him to stay for lunch.

A lunch date became a dinner date, and it quickly turned into regular dating and sizzling sex. After two months, Jim asked Reese to marry him, and without hesitation she agreed, but her parents weren't too fond of Jim because of his drinking habits and career. Despite Reese's parents' protests about Jim's worthiness of their daughter, they eventually subdued their objections about the couple because they loved Reese and adored her happiness. They also knew, as do most parents, that the stronger their disapproval the stronger Reese's defiance grew. And Reese's parents decided that Reese and Jim would wed at the family's estate; they also paid for the honeymoon to Paris as a wedding present.

CHAPTER TWO

THE WEDDING DAY finally arrived. Everything was perfect; the beautiful spring weather was cooperating even though the weatherman called for sixty percent chance of showers. Reese's bridesmaids looked like angels; the table settings were exquisite; the food was Jenny Craig's worst nightmare, and the BRIDE and GROOM looked like they'd stepped out of a magazine cover photo shoot. Everything was truly PERFECT, or so Reese thought.

Just three hours into the reception, everyone noticed Jim's elaborately preposterous behavior as he consumed alcohol at an alarming rate. Jim and John flirted with the bridesmaids, the female caterers, and Jim even had the nerve to flirt with Reese's mother.

Although Reese observed Jim's ravenous appetite for cougar attention and thought she had mistakenly married the wrong man, she became aroused by his masculinity, as Jim, her husband of only three hours, disappeared into the guesthouse with one of the female caterers. Reese's composure turned to embarrassment, yet she took it in stride and continued mingling with her guests. If years of etiquette had taught Reese anything, it was that a real lady never lets her anxiety show.

After the reception, Reese retreated to her room. The day was long, and she was tired and confused. She wondered out loud how in the hell her new husband could cheat on her in her own home---the place where she grew up, had family dinners, and holidays. Reese became so enraged that she couldn't hold it any longer. The images of seeing her husband flirt with women at their wedding finally spewed over, and an inner voice spoke. Then Reese's inner voice manifested into a person, and that person sat beside her. Reese saw what appeared to be her mirror image; she thought, "Am I having an out of body experience, like Shirley McClain spoke of all these years?" Reese studied the figure as it blinked, breathed, and began moving as a real, living being. Reese contributed her hallucination to exhaustion and stress as she continued to examine her twin despite feeling a little foolish. Given Reese's medical training, she thoroughly questioned her sanity. Then the entity glared at Reese and said, "No, you're not cracking up. And hell yeah *WE* could use a drink!"

A dazed Reese glided toward the wet bar in the corner of her room, poured a glass of Scotch with no ice, downed it, and then poured another shot hoping it would calm her nerves, but it didn't. Reese turned around hoping that the image was gone, and when she didn't see it on the bed she sighed and thought that that was too damn freaky for comfort, and then the image appeared and uttered, "I know that was some freaky shit, huh? I've been waiting for quite some time to present myself to you." Reese spun around to locate the image sitting with its legs crossed on the LOUIS XVI armchair in a corner of the room with a glass which appeared to be the same drink Reese held. "So! What are *WE* planning to do about Jim's alcoholic, cheating ass? Can't believe that asshole has luscious beauty, brains, and money, and he STILL fucks up!" An unresponsive Reese observed the image, and without a word Reese tilted her head back and gulped her drink. The Scotch scalded Reese's throat and stomach lining causing her to wince in temporary agony and then in buzzed satisfaction. Reese gathered her senses and spoke, "Okay *ME*, what shall I call *ME*?" Without hesitation the image said, "RITA. *YOU* can call *ME*…RITA."

At that point the roar of a commotion arose from downstairs, and Reese overheard her parents screaming at someone. Then Jim's distinguishable voice shouted, "FUCK YOU!" Jim stormed inside the room where Reese still wore her adorned bridal gown. Reese silently stood in the middle of the bedroom with an empty glass in her hand. Jim spoke, but his voice sounded distant to Reese; she wasn't answering back, and in frustration Jim took off his tux while she stared at him as if in a trance. Jim threw his jacket, tie, and pants across the room but struggled with the buttons on his shirt; he cursed and collapsed on the bed butt-naked from the waist down. Jim immediately fell into a deep slumber and snored loud enough to disturb the Western Hemisphere.

Reese stood over Jim and gaped down at him first with hatred because he ruined their wedding day, and then with murderous disdain since the prick consummated their marriage with a slutty caterer whom Reese's parents had essentially paid to screw her husband. The icing on the cake was missing their flight to Paris. Reese desperately yearned to explore the Catacombs de Paris and The

Louvre, but Reese knew that trip would likely be postponed indefinitely.

Reese's temper slowly subsided, and Rita appeared next to Reese glaring at Jim and slowly shook her head then disappeared without a word. Reese went to the other side of the bed, and without taking off her bridal gown lay down next to her husband, looked into his face, and convinced herself that her emotions were only based on assumptions, and that Jim hadn't cheated on her on their wedding day. That's when Rita whispered, "Right, Bitch. And I'm not real. Uh huh." Reese also disregarded her illogical conversation because she was a well-known psychiatrist who had published several books and papers, and then with a smirk, she blamed it on the long chaotic day and fell asleep.

After days of make-up sex and relaxation, Reese went back to work in her downtown Boston office, and Jim went back to his job with the Police Department. Since the wedding fiasco, Jim apologized numerous times and denied that he'd slept with anyone on their wedding night, and he promised to quit drinking. Reese believed him. So, they moved on like nothing happened.

Given their hectic schedules, Reese and Jim managed to gather for lunch every day at Reese's office, and the two would carelessly have sex in her office knowing that her secretary could hear everything. One afternoon, Jim brought up the subject of kids and again begged Reese to take his last name, but Reese wasn't interested in having kids and was adamant about maintaining her father's last name. Reese came from an old, aristocratic family, so her name was her identity, and she wanted to keep it. The couple constantly argued about having a family of their own, but having kids wasn't in Reese's current plans because she anally wanted to accomplish her list of goals. Reese's stubbornness infuriated Jim; he didn't want to accept her decision, so he stormed out without another word. Reese was stunned, yet a minute piece of her admired Jim's persistence—little did she know that that conversation, which started out peaceful, would become a declaration of war. Once more she contemplated her decision to marry Jim, and then in a barely audible whisper a voice said, "Divorce his monkey ass." Reese shook it off and went to her computer to review her patients' cases for the next day.

Six hours later the hard rain outside turned to sleet and began to hit the window. Reese worried about Jim, and a sickening feeling developed inside her stomach. Reese didn't know what it was from, "Could've been some Chinese food from earlier," she contemplated to herself before drawing her thoughts back to Jim. Reese assumed that Jim was probably at a bar drowning his frustration; although she prayed he wasn't, so she shook her head and returned to her cases.

Later that night Jim came home, stormed into the bedroom, and stumbled around smelling as if he crawled out of a tank of beer. Slurring his words while trying to say something intelligible he bellowed, "IF YYYOU DONNNN WANNN MY LASSSSS NNNNAAAAMMMMMEEEE, TTTHHHHANNN

YOU RRIISSHHH AAAASSSS IS GIMME ME A BABY GOSH DAMINT!" Jim grabbed Reese's arms, held her down, and injected his penis inside of her. Jim pumped feverishly and tried to kiss Reese, but a disgusted, astonished Reese cried and turned her head then released a whimpered, "No!" as her husband continued to have sex with her. Reese tried to scream, but something inside prevented her. Reese thought, "How am I being raped by my own husband?" Jim moaned and trembled when he climaxed. Jim forced himself off of Reese, and he stumbled away leaving his wife on the bed sobbing and quivering. Jim staggered down the stairs and out the house into the cold, freezing rain. Jim's tires screeched into the dark night like a banshee chasing prey.

Miles away from home Jim began to sober and he called John crying still slurring his words a bit. Jim tried wiping the stinging tears away from his face as he told John of his exploits with Reese. While on the phone, a distraught Jim wasn't paying attention to the ice that built up on the road and hit an ice patch. He lost control of his car and went over a cliff. His car exploded on impact. The Police Captain of the famed Boston Police Department for over 25 years perished in the smoldering heat and metal.

About an hour later Reese lay on the bed still crying and shaking. Reese heard the phone ring and hesitated answering it because she thought it was Jim, but after examining the caller I.D. she answered. "Reese? It's John. Honey…I've got some real bad news. Jim has had a car accident." Reese unemotionally received the news of her husband's demise; she hung up the phone and made her way to the bathroom where she began cramping and bleeding. The pain buckled Reese's knees, and she collapsed on the floor shrieking and screaming in pain. Upon hearing the screams from Reese's room, her parents ran up the stairs. They didn't see Reese, so Mrs. Withers called out to her daughter, and after hearing moaning sounds coming from the bathroom, Mr. Withers ran over to the door and opened it to discover Reese on the bathroom floor in a fetal position lying in a pool of blood. Mrs. Withers screamed and rushed over to her daughter while Mr. Withers ran to the hallway and yelled for someone to call an ambulance. Then Mr. Withers returned to the bathroom to care for his ailing daughter.

When the EMTs arrived, they assessed and sedated Reese then strapped her to a gurney for the ride to Mercy Hospital. When the EMS ambulance arrived at the hospital, doctors and nurses were eagerly waiting in the emergency bay. An EMT opened the back door to retrieve Reese, and the staff hurriedly rolled her into a trauma room followed by Mr. and Mrs. Withers who had followed the ambulance in their Bentley.

After an hour or so in a private waiting room, Dr. Karen Smith appeared wearing a bloody smock and approached Mr. and Mrs. Withers who were joined by some of the estate staff who were keeping a vigil. After hearing the update of Reese's condition, a fragile Mrs. Withers sobbed uncontrollably while Mr. Withers tried to catch her before she fell to the floor. Mr. Withers only words were, "Pregnant…are you sure? How many weeks was she?" Dr. Smith reported that Reese had been in her first trimester before the miscarriage. Dr. Smith also reported the presence of some unexplained injuries to the back of Reese's head resulting in brain trauma.

As Dr. Smith exited the private waiting area, another doctor approached Mr. Withers to notify him of Jim's death. A shocked Mr. Withers asked the doctor how his son-in-law died, but the doctor instructed him to contact the detective conducting the investigation and told him that Jim's remains were in the morgue when the family was ready to release them to a mortuary. Mr. Withers replied, "I never liked that son-of-a-bitch, but damn it to hell he was my daughter's husband, so I guess I've got to find a way to deal with this." Mr. Withers hesitated breaking the morbid news to his wife. "Shit," thought Mr. Withers. He shook the doctor's hand and gave him leave. Mr. Withers sucked up some fresh air, blew it out, and then walked over to his wife and told her about Jim.

CHAPTER THREE

2011: REESE woke up about 6:30am on a

Monday morning out of a heavy slumber feeling groggy and drained. It was the two year anniversary of Reese's tragic nightmare with Jim, Jim's accident, and her miscarriage. And it was also Reese's first day back to work. She slowly pulled the blankets off, put both legs over the edge of the bed, and let them dangle. Reese muttered to herself, "Let's get a move on girl; you have new patients to see, and a new car to drive." That thought perked Reese up right away. Reese contemplated drinking a 5 hour energy drink but decided against it because she concluded it was full of unhealthy additives that made it taste like shit. Reese got up from her bed, went into the bathroom, and started her shower. While the water warmed, Reese went over to the sink to brush her teeth and put on a facial mask. She could see the hot mist create a thin fog over the mirror which confirmed that the temperature of the water was ready for her shower.

After 20 minutes Reese stepped out feeling refreshed and ready for the day. Reese left the bathroom and found a silver tray of English muffins, lightly buttered, with a side of strawberry jam and a cup of black coffee on her wet bar. Reese smiled to herself and said aloud, "God bless you Mrs. Henderson." Mrs. Henderson was the Withers' house manager and had been with the family for over four decades. Reese took a bite of an English muffin, a sip of coffee, and turned her attention to her closet to select an outfit, but then she noticed that

Mrs. Henderson had already laid out a stunning collaboration of items---a satin, burgundy Chanel business suit Reese picked up while in Italy a few short months ago, satin red wine Jimmy Choo's (Reese owned over 100 of the famed stilettos), a garnet broach worn by her late grandmother at Princess Diana's wedding, and a black diamond & garnet necklace. Reese wore her three carat diamond earrings every day and insisted on wearing her wedding ring despite being a widow. After dressing and accessorizing, Reese took her shoes out of the box, sat down on a bench inside the closet, and put them on. Then she stood up, looked in the full-length mirror, and said, "DAMN GIRL! NOT BAD AT ALL…NOT AT ALL!"

    Reese went over to her desk, picked up manila folders containing her new patients' information, two boxes of pens, and her cell phone and put them in her briefcase. Reese grabbed her FENDI bag and her car keys and left the bedroom. Reese departed down the spiral staircase to the foyer and left the house. Reese's car was waiting for her already warmed up thanks to Michael who was in charge of all the family's transportation. Reese opened the passenger side door, laid her briefcase on the seat, and closed the door. When Reese opened the driver's door she inhaled the new car smell. This was her baby, a brand new Audi R8 GT; she snobbishly took pride in the fact that only 333 R8s were made, and she had one. Reese wasn't into all the specification of the beast, but the AUDI salesman said that the R8 GT contained a 5.5 liter V10 engine that produced over 533 horsepower. Now Reese really didn't know what that meant, but when she took it on a test drive the engine was so powerful that Reese swore she had an orgasm because her panty shield was soaking wet.

Reese put her driving gloves on and turned the radio to Sports Center on Sirius/XM to listen to what her boy toy Tom Brady and the Patriots were doing. Reese had followed the New England Patriots since she was a little girl. Reese's dad was a long time suite owner, and she cherished memories of games at the old Sullivan Stadium despite her dislike of watching football during a blizzard. Yet, she enjoyed spending time with her father. Reese returned her focus to driving and sped away from the family's estate going 50 mph. "Thank God the family owns the private road." Reese thought as neared the public cross street and merged with traffic. Reese headed to the freeway going east on 90 to downtown Boston; the whole trip took less than 45 minutes without traffic and about an hour with traffic, but Reese hoped her new car would shave off 10-15 minutes of travel time.

Arriving at the John Hancock building at exactly 9:00 am, Reese drove up to the third floor of the parking garage specifically marked for each suite owner; she parked in her assigned spot. Reese turned the engine off and sat in her car a moment recalling that she hadn't been there in almost two years. Reese tried not to dwell on the past, so she retrieved her belongings from the passenger seat and got out of her car. She clicked the alarm button and walked to the bay of elevators. While walking Reese couldn't help cautiously examining her surroundings because she nervously expected someone to jump out and grab her, so she walked at an accelerated pace. As Reese approached the bay, the elevator doors opened instantly. A bit startled Reese glanced around before walking into the elevator. Reese pushed the button for the twenty-first floor, and the doors closed. The music in the elevator was soft and soothing, and Reese guessed it was R. Kelly's, "I BELIEVE I CAN FLY," so she started to hum.

Reese's floor came rather quickly because it was an express elevator, and it only stopped on odd number floors. Reese exited and walked to her office suite. It seemed so surreal to Reese; she had a bustling practice with over one hundred patients, and now it appeared that she was starting over again like when she graduated from college. There were butterflies in her stomach, and she questioned returning to her practice. She didn't need the money…money she had, but helping people drove Reese to continue her work. Reese stuck her hand out to touch the name plate on the door. It read, DR. MONICA WITHERS, Ph.D. "God I missed this place." Reese took the keys out of her purse and unlocked her office suite. Reese stepped into the lobby, turned off the alarm, and then opened a secret panel behind the rubber plant. Inside there were a series of numbers and buttons. Reese pushed a couple of numbers on the control panel to turn on the new hidden camera system that she had a security company install a few weeks prior. The new system allowed Reese to see and hear everything that occurred in the office, the lobby, and her private bathroom which turned into a Panic Room if need be. The system also tracked the receptionist's phone calls, emails, web surfing, all document reading, altering, and sharing, and copy machine usage. Reese could monitor the system from her smart phone or from a computer anywhere in world. Reese contemplated her paranoia and need for these gadgets, and she considered taking medication to calm her nerves, but Reese's dad convinced her that the added security was in her best interest. Reese closed the panel, walked through the lobby to her office, and opened the door. Reese went straight to her desk, put down her purse, and her briefcase, and then she walked over to the windows and pulled the shades open. The view of the Boston skyline was beautiful; her view overlooked the Charles River, and she could see people walking and jogging around the river and sailboats moving up and down the river at a snail's pace. She diverted her attention to her Rolex and anticipated her new receptionist's arrival any moment.

Reese went to her private bathroom to check her appearance and came back into the office where she was startled by another person's presence. After a few quick breaths, Reese realized that it was her new receptionist, Maria. Maria was also startled and apologized to Reese, "I'm so sorry Dr. Withers. I saw your door open and called out, but you didn't answer, so I walked in to ascertain your whereabouts and introduce my presence."

Reese recovered quickly and said, "No, no! Don't worry about it. I didn't hear you. My mind was on other things. Good to see you. I appreciate your punctuality. In fact, I'm a stickler for it." Reese extended her hand to shake Maria's hand and guided Maria to her desk in the lobby. Reese reminded Maria of her personal do's and don'ts of professionalism in addition to the basic legal rules and regulations of a psychiatric office. Reese gave Maria a set of keys to the office and the alarm code, but Reese did not tell Maria about the additional security system that stayed on twenty four hours a day.

What Reese learned about Maria from their initial interview was that Maria was 5'5" and weighed about a 135 pounds; she was from Miami and moved to Springfield with her now ex-husband who still resided in Western Mass. Maria didn't elaborate on why they got a divorce, but Reese inferred from her tone and the pain on her face that domestic violence was most likely a part of the reason. Maria had no children and no property to speak of, and her chief desire was to make enough money to buy a house and pay off all her debts. Despite Maria's lack of experience directly related to psychiatry, Reese felt bad for her and promised that she would help Maria get back on her feet as soon as possible.

Ten a.m. arrived, and so did Reese's first patient. Maria informed Reese that Mrs. Alice Clayton waited in the lobby. So, Reese rose from her desk, opened the closet door, and felt flushed by what she saw in the mirror. Reese expected to see her calm, confident reflection in the mirror, but she was startled instead by Rita's expression. "This proves it!" Reese whispered aloud. "I'm not a well person. Why are you here, Rita? It is Rita isn't it?"

Rita looked back at Reese with such disdain that Rita couldn't help to contain herself. "Look Bitch!" said Rita in a low, confrontational voice. "Once you learn to accept the fact that I exist, the better off you'll be! But if you keep denying me I guarantee that I'll have your ass dreaming of SERTA SHEEPS butt raping you every time you take a nap or go to bed at night!" To which Reese replied, "Damn. That was kind of graphic; I like those cute sheep on the commercials. You must be my alter ego. Some version of myself I've created due to trauma…right?"

    Rita smirked, "You're the psychiatrist not me. And I know you like those lame fucking sheep. That's why I said it."

    Reese looked at Rita in the mirror and asked, "Why are you here?"

Rita replied, "I'll answer all your questions later, but first you have to deal with the crazy ass coot in the lobby."

Puzzled at that statement, Reese looked at Rita and said, "What do you know of my first patient?"

To which Rita responded, "Don't worry about it sweetheart. I have everything under control."

"What aren't you telling me about this patient? And why aren't you revealing what you know about me?" Reese demanded.

But Rita calmly inquired, "By the way, how do I look in this outfit? Does it make my butt look fat?" With an inquisitive smile Rita said nothing and closed the closet door. "I'm still here dumb ass." Rita said annoyed, but

Reese ignored her final comment and headed for the lobby to retrieve Mrs. Clayton.

After quickly freshening her make-up, Reese walked into the main lobby where sat an older woman in her mid to late sixties dressed impeccably tastefully. One could tell by looking at Mrs. Clayton that she came from either old money or was married to it. There was a stiff air of supercilious confidence in Mrs. Clayton's face. Reese concluded that Mrs. Clayton, despite her age, was very striking. Mrs. Clayton was voluptuous with nice curves, and one could most definitely tell that she worked out at least three times a week. Reese extended her hand to shake Mrs. Clayton's hand, but Mrs. Clayton without one word bitterly walked past Reese and into Reese's office. Reese looked at Maria, and Maria leaned over and whispered,

"She hasn't spoken one word to me besides telling me her name, and that she had a ten o'clock appointment with you. And then she just sat there staring at me and waiting." Reese shrugged her shoulders, walked back into her office, and shut the door behind her. Reese had an eerie feeling that Rita knew something awful about Mrs. Clayton that she wasn't disclosing.

As Reese walked to the other side of her desk, she continued to ponder Rita's knowledge of her new client as she inquired whether Mrs. Clayton would be more comfortable on the couch. Mrs. Clayton coldly responded that she was comfortable where she was, took off her white gloves, and ran her index finger along Reese's desk. Mrs. Clayton glanced around the office admiring the tasteful decor. Reese peered at Mrs. Clayton as she grabbed a new yellow legal pad to annotate what she was witnessing. In big letters Reese wrote CONTROL FREAK TO THE 10th POWER and circled it. "Is everything to your liking Mrs. Clayton?"

"I see by looking around your office Dr. Withers that you're a woman of great taste." Mrs. Clayton snobbishly replied and continued to scan the office as if she was coming back late at night to rob the place.

"How may I help you this morning Mrs. Clayton?"

"I was referred to you by an associate to speak with you about an issue that I have. And I don't know if I'm ashamed of it or just being a foolish woman."

"Okay, where would you like to begin, Mrs. Clayton? You may start where ever you like."

Mrs. Clayton shifted uncomfortably in her seat then looked at the couch and decided to move there. Reese noted the transition on her legal pad, moved to a love seat opposite of Mrs. Clayton, and waited patiently for her to speak. When Mrs. Clayton found her comfort spot, she looked at Reese with steel blue eyes and spoke. "Well Dr. Withers, I presume you've read about my husband, Senator Richard Gregory Clayton III, and have heard about my business affairs with your father." Reese recalled a few details about Mrs. Clayton's high profile life. She remembered Mrs. Clayton was ranked as one of the most powerful women in the country, and that her husband was the Majority Senate Leader, and he was also considered one of the most powerful people in the country. Hell, Reese thought that she'd read somewhere that Mr.

Clayton was more powerful than the President of the United States given Mr. Clayton's political connections and money. Although Mr. Clayton refused to run for the Presidency because he was quoted in the New York Times as saying, "Congress is full of shit, and the bastards should die a horrible death." When asked about it on the television program called Face the Nation, the reporter asked Mr. Clayton if his words were taken out of context to which Mr. Clayton replied, "Fuck NO! Hell yeah I said it, and I'll say it again." Everyone was so shocked that the producer couldn't find the beep button to edit out the curse words.

Reese annotated that she wanted to conduct further research into Senator Clayton's life and work. Then she turned her attention back to Mrs. Clayton who asked, "I'm assuming that whatever I say in these sessions is confidential? What's the saying dear…Doctor-Patient privilege?"

"Yes, Mrs. Clayton. Everything that you say remains between you and I and is considered privileged information in court. I am ethically bound to keep your trust. So please continue." Reese confirmed.

"Had to be sure, I don't want my business all over the trash TV. Anyway, doctor I've been having an extra martial affair for the past 2-3 years. And it's not with a man but with another woman…a much younger woman." Mrs. Clayton spewed.

Reese showed no sign of emotion but inside her head she could see Rita laughing hysterically. Reese concentrated on Mrs. Clayton and continued to annotate in Mrs. Clayton's file. Reese could feel the laughter building inside her to the point that Reese's face was starting to show signs of amusement. Mrs. Clayton, who wasn't paying attention to Reese's new facial expression, continued to speak. "Please don't misunderstand me doctor. I still enjoy a stiff one once in a while, but I just find the company of women more satisfying. My orgasms reach a plateau that no man has ever climbed." Reese asked Mrs. Clayton to describe the type of relationship she had with her husband and the last time they had sex. Then Reese encouraged Mrs. Clayton to elaborate on the relationship she shared with her lover. Mrs. Clayton did not blush at the question, yet the tone of Reese's voice irritated her. Yet, Mrs. Clayton managed to force a calm response, "I haven't had sex with my husband in almost three years, and I had sex with my lover before I came to see you." Mrs. Clayton's tone was as if she were offering a cube of sugar for tea.

Reese continued, "Does your husband know about your affair, Mrs. Clayton?" Mrs. Clayton scoffed and shrugged her narrow shoulders as if to say: what if he did; what the hell he is going to do about it; not a damn thing. Reese asked Mrs. Clayton about the real reason she'd scheduled an appointment since she wasn't distraught about her affair or her marriage. Reese felt like Mrs. Clayton harbored a clandestine motive, and she wanted to shout, "Get on with it! I'm not your priest; this isn't confession. If you want me to help you work out your problems then let's work! Stop toying with me! This isn't an episode of Dynasty!" Reese inhaled and composed herself then asked Mrs. Clayton if she was planning to divorce her husband. Mrs. Clayton didn't hesitant with her answer. "No! I don't plan to divorce Richard, and furthermore I like the way things are between us." Reese inquired if Mrs. Clayton planned to confront her husband with the truth of the affair. Mrs. Clayton dramatically shifted and looked at Reese as if she took the last slice of cheesecake; then she replied, "How stupid do you think I am? Are you that naturally fucked for brains?"

Reese was irritated with this woman and withheld her response to Mrs. Clayton's snide remark. Instead Reese continued annotating and glanced at the clock praying that the hour was nearing an end. "Good," Reese whispered and smiled. "Ten more minutes left to get this

horrible woman out of my office and hopefully my life."
Reese didn't want to start back to work with this type of case. Mrs. Clayton witnessed Reese's glance at the clock and the smirk on her face. So, Mrs. Clayton started to gather her things and stated, "You're probably wondering why I came to see you today Dr. Withers. Trust me. It isn't for your psychological journal either but to reintroduce myself to you." Reese stopped writing and stared at Mrs. Clayton like a deer at headlights. Mrs. Clayton deviously continued, "I would like to talk to you about your late husband, Jim."

An infuriated Reese said, "What the hell do you know of my husband, Mrs. Clayton?"

Mrs. Clayton sneered, "You still don't remember me do you doctor? I met you at your wedding…at your family's estate. We shook hands, and we chit chatted for a couple of minutes. I remember you being distracted during our conversation because you were watching Jim flirt with every woman at the reception. I saw him flirting too doctor, especially with a blond servant girl who was serving drinks that evening. We both watched Jim disappear with that woman into the guesthouse. You looked at me, and I saw a little hint of a tear form in the corner of your eye, but like a debutante you continued to mingle with your guests. Then I watched you leave the reception, so I walked towards the guesthouse in search of Jim and the servant. When I got there I retrieved my cell phone and took pictures of your husband screw her like a dog in heat. She moaned so loud it was shocking that no one else heard them. Well I was clicking away until the blonde opened her eyes and yelped. Jim, with his pants around his ankles, suddenly stopped and turned around to find me standing in the doorway with my camera phone. As Jim reached for his pants, he pleaded with me not to tell anyone. I told him to drop his pants. The servant girl cried profusely and also begged me to keep it a secret because she was worried about losing her job. Stupid blonde also confessed that she had a sick kid like I gave a crap. I told her to give me her name and number, and I promised we would work something out. Well that hoe hurried out of the guesthouse, and Jim stood there cupping his genitals like that character from "OLIVER TWIST" begging 'Please, sir can I have more!' Doctor as I approached your husband I told his whorish ass that I wanted him to fuck me the same voracious way he fucked her, and if I didn't moan like that blonde bitch that I'd send those pictures to you. So just like a dog on command your husband commenced into me like a SWAT team breaking down a door in a drug raid."

Reese couldn't believe what she was hearing from this woman. "Is she actually saying that she fucked my husband at my wedding and filmed it?" Reese could feel herself lose all touch of reality. Reese felt the inside of her body going into warp speed and within seconds Reese was in a trance-like state. Reese was no longer present; her body was there, but her consciousness was replaced with her alter ego, Rita. Rita continued to listen to Mrs. Clayton who didn't know that Rita was calculating a revengeful plan of action. Rita contemplated Mrs. Clayton's destruction because she knew that the malevolent T-Rex's demise shouldn't be traceable to Reese.

Mrs. Clayton stood at the door with her hand on the door knob and asked Reese, "Are you wondering why I'm telling you this doctor…today being your first day back to your practice and all? Judging by the 'I just pissed the bed' look on your face all this news seems kind of a shock. Well I tell you dear, your father and I were entering a deal of massive proportions. We were going to merge our two companies to become the largest rail and fleet company in the world. Your father and I both stood to make billions. The lawyers spent countless billable hours constructing the paperwork, and I was ready for us to sign and finalize the merger when your father pulled out and merged with a European company. Of course that pissed me off! I lost millions pursuing that deal! And to have your pompous ass father pull my tampon out from under me and not give me an opportunity to counter the European offer or offer me an explanation as to why he rejected my deal was too much of a bitch move. Well you know I just couldn't let that slide. So of course, I was shocked to receive an invite for your wedding, yet I had to take the opportunity to say FUCK YOU, very much to your father, you, and your new family. But…who knew that night would be so magical." Mrs. Clayton finally opened the door and said, "I'll let myself out. Don't worry dear. I'll pay the bill before I leave." And Mrs. Clayton's final surprise for Reese was implementing herself in Jim's death by asking whether or not the police ever checked Jim's brakes. "What an unfortunate accident--very unfortunate indeed, but good dick though." Mrs. Clayton walked out the office and closed the door behind her leaving Reese frozen in a trance-like state, while Rita took the brunt of Mrs. Clayton's tirade.

Rita had taken over Reese's subconscious to protect her from more psychological damage. Rita knew that Mrs. Clayton had to be removed from the earth SOON, and Rita needed to meticulously plan how she was going to do it. For Reese's well-being Rita would have to erase the conversation with Mrs. Clayton and plant pleasant thoughts. Rita prevented Reese from ease-dropping while she maliciously continued to conceive a plan that CSI couldn't solve in an hour. Eventually Rita brought Reese back from her dream-like state by calling her name, "REESE…REESE…WAKE UP YOU CRAZY

BITCH." Reese blinked her eyes and looked around her office wondering where Mrs. Clayton went. Reese looked at her clock and saw that the session was over, and Reese couldn't remember anything from Mrs. Clayton's session besides that Mrs. Clayton was a Lesbian and a Control freak. Reese looked down at her legal pad, reread her notes, and filed it.

Since Reese hit her head in her bathroom two years ago, she suffered from recurring migraines. Reese looked in her medicine cabinet for Imitrex and saw that there weren't any. Reese asked Maria to take one of the three office cars and pick up a refill from the drugstore. Reese pointed towards the beige storage box on the wall by the closet door. Maria opened the storage box and stared at three keys to a Black 2011 Chrysler 300 Sedan, a Black

2010 Chevy Impala, and a Black 2011 Chevy Camaro. Maria selected the marked key ring for the 2011 Chevy Camaro and verified the location of the vehicle. Maria felt a rush of excitement since she had never driven a Camaro or anything made after 2000. "Hell it's 100 times better than the piece of shit El Camino my father gave me 12 years ago," Maria thought. Reese gave Maria one hundred dollars for the medication and told Maria to get whatever she wanted with the change. Maria said thank you, left Reese's office, and closed the door behind her. Reese watched Maria leave and decided to lay down for a quick nap. Maria pocketed her cell phone, and then she grabbed her purse and coat from the closet and left the office. Maria locked the outer office door, headed for the elevators, took out her cell phone, and pushed the preset number "2" for the NATIONAL REPORTER. The NATIONAL REPORTER was a third tier tabloid with over 150,000 subscribers. The elevator arrived; Maria stepped in and pushed the number three on the panel. The door closed, and with the phone to her ear Maria listened to the ring tone and waited for someone to pick up on the other line. A man with a loud baritone voice yelled, "EDITOR"S DESK." Maria knew that her boss of five years was famous for loathing nonessential bullshit, so Maria quickly reported her first day discoveries while working for Dr. Monica Withers. The Editor listening to the news damn near had an erection when he heard her notes on one of the country's most powerful women, Mrs. Alice Clayton. The Editor told Maria to continue to gather all the information she could on Mrs. Clayton and

Dr. Withers. The Editor told Maria to plant a listening device in Dr. Withers office so that Maria could listen and tape the psychiatric sessions. The Editor commended Maria on her good work and assured her that if she could get the complete story that the promotion she'd been begging for would be all hers. Maria stepped out of the elevator and disconnected the call; she put the phone into her purse and pulled out the keys in search of the Camaro. The key ring read 3rd floor, section 2B. Maria walked to that section and found the Camaro. She thought, "Damn! I wish this was my car! Shit I can pick up any man in this dick wagon." Maria opened the car door and slide inside. She put the key into the ignition, turned it, and revved the engine like a new vibrator fresh out of the box. Maria giggled hearing the engine growl and then remembered that she was running an errand for her rich ass boss.

Forty minutes later Maria returned with Reese's medicine and gave Reese the change. Reese said thank you, and Maria returned the key back to the storage box. Reese went into the bathroom to take her medicine. Maria, seizing her opportunity, planted listening devices under Reese's desk and behind the file cabinet. Reese entered the office and told Maria that she was done for the day then requested her prompt return in the morning. Maria asked if Reese was sure, and Reese said yes and assured Maria she would get paid for the whole day. Maria said her goodbyes and left the office locking the outer office door. Reese sat at her and felt dizzy again. Reese thought it might have been a reaction to her medication, but she was slightly skeptical because she'd been taking the medicine for the past two years. So, Reese decided to lay down on the couch to rest. Shortly thereafter Reese fell asleep.

CHAPTER FOUR

As Reese slumbered, Rita awoke. Rita got up from the couch and went into the bathroom to wash up. Rita still seethed over that Leona Helmsley bitch of a woman, Mrs. Clayton; Rita wanted to give Mrs. Clayton a planet size ass kicking, and Rita already had a plan set in motion. Rita knew that Mrs. Clayton would get hers in the long run, but she needed to be patient. Rita walked back into the office, opened the closet door, and changed her clothes. Rita picked out a burgundy trench coat, a black cashmere turtleneck sweater, black BLEULAB jeans, and black knee high boots. Looking in the mirror Rita touched her hips and resolved that she had to put Reese on a freaking diet because the heifer was killing their figure. Rita moved some of the blouses that were hanging up out of her way and pushed a panel on the wall which revealed a couple of stylish wigs, sunglasses, a voice translator, and her favorite Desert Eagle .40. Rita picked up the long, heavy gun and caressed it like a lost lover. She chambered a round in the weapon and stored it in the inside pocket of her trench coat. Rita picked up more ammo and an untraceable cell phone. Rita turned the cell phone on and within minutes it revealed 12 messages---ten of which came from that nasty bitch Mrs. Clayton. Rita's Grinch grin said, "It's time to play."

Rita went to the storage box, snatched the keys to the 2011 Chrysler 300 Sedan, and left the office. Rita went to the third floor, and as she opened the car door, she noticed someone lurking between the pillars. Whoever it was didn't notice Rita getting into the car. So, Rita patiently sat in the driver's seat to catch a glimpse of the person sneaking around, and then the figure came into view. Rita smiled and said, "Now ain't this about a bitch." The mysterious person was the blond caterer who fucked Jim at the reception. "What was her name?" Rita contemplated. "Oh, yes! I remember! That tramp's name is Tara. Damn idiot! What the hell is she doing in Reese's office building? She must have followed Mrs. Clayton." Rita noticed that the stupid bitch had a cell phone in her hand and was taking pictures of the cars. Rita continued to watch Tara. Rita picked up her cell phone, connected the voice translator, placed the phone on the car mount, and waited.

Tara hid behind pillars sticking her head out periodically as if to ambush someone. Tara's phone rang startling the dimwit, and she almost dropped the phone. Tara thought she'd silenced the ringer. Looking at the cell phone screen, she noticed the caller was that controlling bitch Mrs. Alice Clayton. Tara knew to answer the phone before the second ring, so she pushed the answer button and said in a cherry voice as she rolled her eyes, "Hello mommy." That's what Alice wanted Tara to call her at all times, in bed, in public…anywhere. That was Alice's rule. If Tara didn't abide by it then Alice wouldn't give her any shopping money or pay her rent. Tara was sick of Alice's control. Tara continued, "Yes mommy. I'll be at the hotel within thirty minutes. Yes! I'm not wearing any panties!" The other line abruptly hung up leaving Tara to look at her phone and say, "Bitch!"

Tara had plans for Mrs. Alice Clayton. Tara was going to black mail that crusty ass bitch of a whore back to the Stone Ages. Since Tara's encounter with Alice at the wedding reception, Alice held ALL the cards. Mrs. Clayton threatened Tara every chance she got. "I'm the boss! And if my shit affects your delicate nasal passage I WILL CANCEL you faster than a FOX television show. Just ask SETH MCFARLANE." At first Tara was afraid of Alice because of Alice's wealth and stature, but over time Tara became irritated and frustrated by Alice's arrogance. Tara's plan involved recording anything and everything she and Alice did together. Tara even contacted a reporter---a Maria Bradshaw at the NATIONAL REPORTER--- to sell the information if Mrs. Clayton didn't agree to Tara's new terms. Tara had voice recordings from the first year she and Alice were together, and once Tara overheard Alice in the bathroom talking softly to someone on the phone about fixing someone's car, how she wanted it to look like an accident, and wanted it done ASAP. Tara collected the info and stored some of it at her apartment and in another safe location.

Without realizing that she was also being watched, Tara began to walk down to the first floor of the garage. Rita took photo stills of Tara's actions. Then Rita lifted up the cell, pushed a preset number, and waited for a connection.

Sitting in the back seat of her chauffeured limousine Mrs. Clayton was thinking about what transpired at Dr. Withers office. Mrs. Clayton didn't notice it then, but now that she had time to think about it she remembered something odd about Dr. Withers facial expression. As Mrs. Clayton's words were tearing Monica's asshole like paper, she grasped that Monica stood there taking the verbal abuse without attacking her and there was something disturbing about Monica's cold, empty glare. Mrs. Clayton dared not to describe it. Just then Mrs. Clayton's cell vibrated making her heart skip a beat. She answered the phone with so much venom that it spewed out on the other end, "Where in the FUCK have you been! I've called and left numerous messages! I fucking can't remember how many!" Then she abruptly stopped her tirade and listened intently. With a Wiley coyote grin on her face, she thought everything was again right with the universe. Mrs. Clayton ejected, "I won't miss Tara. I'm bored of her. Take care of everything, and I mean EVERYTHING—not one iota of Tara's being should be recognized by the human eye." Mrs. Clayton pushed disconnect on her phone and imagined how a little whore like Tara from the backwaters of God knows where could attempt to blackmail her. "The little fucker just canceled her own life." Mrs. Clayton chuckled. She felt famished, so she called her driver over the intercom and directed him to a restaurant for a late lunch and cocktails. Mrs. Clayton felt like celebrating.

Back at the John Hancock parking garage the Figure in the black Sedan ended the call, started the engine, and set everything in motion after finding Tara's FORD FIESTA a few blocks down the road. The Figure thought that Tara would discover how much she would miss

breathing within the next 30 minutes.

CHAPTER FIVE

Tara, in her late model Ford Fiesta, drove down Main Street listening to the group Three Doors Down. Tara hadn't noticed that she was being trailed by a black Sedan. Tara stopped at a red light on State Street, and the Sedan pulled up beside her on the driver's side. The Figure in the Sedan rolled down the passenger side window and turned up the music on its powerful Bose entertainment system. The music was so loud that the engines on the Space Shuttle would sound muffled in comparison. Tara shaking her head in disgust turned up her music to drain out the noise, but it didn't help. Looking over to see who was driving the car, to give the driver a dirty look, Tara failed to notice a white cargo van pull up on her passenger side. The window on the cargo van's driver's side came down, a long barrel pointed towards Tara's head exited the window, and in a split second a high powered caliber bullet shattered Tara's passenger side window. Then the bullet entered the back of Tara's head, exited her forehead, and spewed brain matter everywhere. Tara's body limped lifelessly against the steering wheel blowing the car horn. The Figure in the black Sedan turned down the music, and the Sedan pulled off casually leaving the scene as the light finally turned green. As the Sedan drove away, the Figure continued to look through the rear view mirror admiring the quickness of the incident. The Figure could see a man jump out of the cargo van's passenger side and run to Tara's car. For extra good measure, the Figure instructed the hired help to put the victim's body on display. So, the man opened the driver's side door and rudely pulled Tara's carcass out onto the street. The cargo van screeched off followed by the Fiesta. The Figure looked down at a Rolex Presidential watch and pushed the stop button on the timer. The whole event took less than 45 seconds.

The Figure called the Client to give an update of the job and mentioned that the next event would take place within the hour. Everything was going according to the Figure's master plan. The Client was really pleased with the way the crew completed the work and offered a bonus for any loose ends. The Figure smiled, thanked the Client, and hung up the phone. The Figure was the first to arrive at the rendezvous location which was an abandoned factory outside of Boston near a river bank. The factory, an old Paper Mill, had been closed for almost twenty years. "Marshes as thick as the Louisiana Bayou are always a good place to blow shit up or to get rid of a body---plus no one travels to the marshland knowing that if they venture back into the marshes they may never leave." The Figure thought.

The Figure waited in the car for the other vehicles to arrive. In the Figure's lap were three envelopes; each was filled with twenty crisp one hundred dollar bills for the three hired helpers. "They were good, very good," concluded the Figure. "I might use them again on a separate gig. Plus I'm going to give them a bonus for doing such good work in a timely manner." The Figure looked at the Rolex and realized that the crew was five minutes late. The Figure didn't like tardiness. "It breeds bad business." Everything the Figure did was according to a meticulous schedule---from eating, sleeping, taking a crap, and believe it or not, sex. Like the Figure's favorite comedian Bernie Mac, may he forever rest in peace, says, "Having sex is like a boxing match. It only takes about 3 minutes for each round. You have 3 minutes to get yours because when I get mine the fight is over." The Figure smiled and noticed two vehicles approaching at a high rate speed. The Figure checked the time again, "15 minutes late." This further soured the Figure's mood.

The vehicles stopped, and the crew got out. Walking towards the Sedan expecting to be paid for a job well done they thought, "Shit not bad for about 45 seconds worth of work." The Figure saw them coming, opened the Sedan's door, and got out. The Figure asked, "Why are you late?" One of the crew immediately replied, "I don't know how to drive a stick shift, so we had to stop to let someone else in the crew drive. Hell and I almost broke off my knee caps driving that piece of shit dune buggy." The crew thought that it was funny as chicken fart, but the Figure was not amused. Before the Figure would pay the help, the crew was ordered to obtain gas cans from the van and pour gas on both the van and the Ford. The crew did as they were told while joking about what they were going to do with their money and hitting each other like kids at the playground. The Figure thought, "Oh fuck this! They can't work for me acting this way. They are too damn immature; plus they have seen my face. They can fight it out in Purgatory." Without a word, the Figure moved in complete and utter silence behind the idiots with a DESERT EAGLE .40 with a laser sight lined and aimed it at one of the crew's head. What happened next happened as fast as pure magic. The Figure aimed at the back of victim #1s head and pulled the trigger splattering his brains and skull parts onto victim 2's clothes and face. Next, the swift, precise marksman aimed and fired at the next victim who was so disoriented he hadn't moved a hair. The bullet blew a crater sized hole through victim # 2's face. Then seeing a perfect sight for victim # 3, the Figure fired through # 2's face into # 3 hitting him in the right eye causing his eye to explode.

The Figure looking at the handy work thought, "With all the other killing I was paid to do I actually would've done these clowns for free." The Figure reached down, lifted the third victim, and put him in the front seat of the cargo van. The Figure poured gas inside and outside of the van, lit a cigarette, and flicked it into the cargo van. The Figure then rushed to put the other two dead as shit morons into the Ford Fiesta and repeated the process. The flames accelerated on both the Ford and the van. The Figure could see the Three Stooge's light up like burnt shit on a stick but didn't want to wait for the explosion. The Figure returned to the Sedan, got in, reached for the stereo, turned on some Carmen, and slowly moved the vehicle away from the camp fire. Within minutes the van went nuclear followed by the Fiesta sending everything upwards and outwards from metal parts to body parts into the river and marshes. The Figure thought, "If anyone tries to investigate the scene it would take "CSI Vegas" and "CSI New York" with the help of "Criminal Minds" at least two months just to drain the marshes…plus it's almost winter! Damn this was good freaking timing. Thank goodness this is real life and not some whacked out want to be first time novelist trying to score a book deal."

CHAPTER SIX

The call came over the police band radio about a homicide and a carjacking that occurred on State Street. Lead Detective John Campbell was having his usual burger and fries at Friday's with his new partner Junior Detective second grade Chyna Taylor from Brooklyn, New York. Chyna decided that she needed a change from all the filth New York City put out every day, plus she disliked dealing with Police politics and knew the Boys Network wouldn't have given her an opportunity to make Detective grade. So, Chyna made the move to the *hated* Land of Boston (because New Yorkers and Bostonians really don't get along with each other especially during FOOTBALL, BASEBALL, and BASKETBALL season). When Chyna found out about the opening in Boston she interviewed for the position and within a week the department offered her the position. Chyna notified her superiors in New York that she was accepting the position and without hesitation her Captain signed off on her transfer.

John hadn't been with a partner since the death of his longtime partner and best friend, Jim Patrick Henry, who tragically died in a car accident two years ago. John missed Jim; even though Jim was his superior, they were like brothers. Bowling, Softball, pickup Basketball games, going to the PATS game...Lord Jim thought, "I missed that man." Following Jim's death, John's new Captain called him into the office to let him know that his mourning days, or in this case John's mourning years, were over and that he would be getting a new partner.

John didn't like it, but he understood. Minutes later the Captain went to his desk and called for Chyna to come in so that John and Chyna could be formally introduced. John first impression of was that she had a lot of spunk and was willing to learn from a veteran such as himself.

John asked for the bill in Friday's restaurant, Chyna left a tip, and they both rushed out the restaurant. Chyna jumped in the passenger seat and answered the call, "12 Bravo in route copy."

Dispatch came back, "Copy 12 Bravo. The M.E. is on site."

Chyna replied, "Copy that command," and Chyna put the mike back into the holder. John turned on the sirens, put the Dodge Interceptor into drive, and drove like a spawn out of hell into traffic. State Street was about 15 minutes away, but the way John was driving they arrived at the crime scene in half the time. The scene was pure chaos; the streets were roped off with yellow cautionary tape as on lookers were trying to get a glimpse of the dead body which was now covered with a white sheet. The Medical Examiner was already taking heat readings on the body to get a time of death for the victim as John and Chyna walked over. John bent down over the victim lifting back the white sheet which was now soaked in blood. Chyna knelling next to her partner looked at the hole in back of the victims head and said, "DAMN!!!! What the fuck!" John looked at Chyna and saw the ghastly look on his partner's face and instructed her to control her emotions because the media was watching. John suggested that Chyna interview the witnesses and make sure that the evidence remained in the chain of custody. Chyna stood up, gathered herself, and did what she was told.

John asked the medical examiner (M.E.), Dr. David Kim, the time of death. Kim replied, "Around two hours ago…maybe three. Do you want to know the cause?" John, looking up at Kim with the expression on his face like he was a freaking idiot replied, "Duh, smart ass."

Dr. Kim smiled and said, "I'm just fucking with you John. The victim died from a big ass hole in the head caused by a big ass bullet from a big ass gun, which by the way we still can't find." John searched the ground for the bullet himself and as he stood up his knees popped. John cursed below his breath and asked Kim to update him on any findings. Kim said that he would.

John turned towards Chyna. And as he walked toward her, it seemed as though time warped. John was no longer walking but flying towards Chyna, and Chyna scattered for cover like Speedy Gonzalez. They were clueless about the origin of the explosion which rocked the city as if it were a meteor fallen from of the sky. John landed on his face and stomach with a "UMMMPHMM" and got the breath knocked out of him. Chyna rushed over to her partner to help him get to cover. John looked up and tried to speak as Chyna shouted, "What the hell was that!"

John finally said, "WHAT THE HELL! WHERE? WHERE?" Chyna responded that she didn't know. John got up, dusted himself off, and regained his composure before running for the car. Chyna followed him as onlookers scrambled, screaming, and running in all directions. John looked up at the cloud of smoke and assumed that it was not far from his current location. When John and Chyna reached the car, they headed to where they assumed the blast originated. The Dodge Interceptor screeched forward burning rubber while the sirens blared to clear other cars which were parked in the middle of the street as onlookers pointed in the direction of the burnt cloud. Chyna stuck her head out the window looking at the smoke to give directions to John. When Chyna and John arrived at the blast their mouths dropped, and they felt sick to their stomachs. The place where John had been an officer since the academy was no longer standing; the station was replaced by a smoldering heap of kindle which looked like it was spread out over three city blocks. John said, "Lord, have sweet mercy on all of us."

Using binoculars, the Figure scanned the ruins. The Figure smiled reminiscing about how easy it was to have the bomb delivered to a secured building. The Figure paid some teenager forty dollars to deliver a package and that was the end of that. The bomb was rigged with a cell phone timer, so all the Figure had to do was call the cell phone inside the package and push the number 5 to start a five minute count down. The package worked to perfection. The Figure called the Client to give an updated report about the disposal of the three garbage bags at the marshlands and the demolishing of the Police Station. The Figure cautiously spoke in prearranged code to avoid Homeland Security interference.

The Client was elated and once again commended the craftiness of the Figure's handiwork. Pleased with a job well done, the Client told the Figure that there would be an extra five hundred thousand dollars in the account. The Figure thanked the client and pushed end on the phone, while bringing up the binoculars to admire the endless commotion of the scene in the commons. The Figure decided to leave the area rather than push the luck of the Irish fearing that someone may think it weird for someone to be looking through binoculars in the middle of the city.

Mrs. Clayton watched the news on television from the back of her Limo. Mrs. Clayton felt more powerful than she ever had; there was a wide smile on her face. The thought of having the power to take a life made her feel rather giddy. Mrs. Clayton was feeling some sort of arousal. This was a first for Mrs. Clayton, not the part of being aroused, but being horny over giving orders to kill. Mrs. Clayton felt wetness and eagerness to do something naughty. Mrs. Clayton looked at her phone to call Tara, but she caught herself before pushing send remembering that Tara was in Hillbilly heaven enjoying some Boone's Farm with her kinfolk. Mrs. Clayton couldn't wait any longer, so she demanded the Limo driver pull over and come to the back of the Limo to tend to her sexual needs. Like a good employee, the driver did as he was told. While the limo driver was screwing his boss, Mrs. Clayton had a thought, a thought of getting rid of that fucking quack doctor, Monica Withers, and then Mrs. Clayton began to moan with ecstasy and climaxed while digging her nails into her faithful employee's back. When Mrs. Clayton was done she told the driver to get back to work, and he did

just as he was told.

CHAPTER SEVEN

It was 7pm. Reese awoke feeling groggy and felt like something was odd. She remembered lying on the couch at work and couldn't recall how she'd gotten home. Reese lay in bed trying to recollect her actions, but her attention was drawn to a reporter interviewing witnesses of the death of a young woman on State Street. Reese wondered how someone could shoot a stranger in the back of the head, leave their body in the middle of the street like garbage, and steal their car. "Jesus." Reese thought.

The next story on the news was of an explosion that leveled two buildings one of which was the police department. The reporter at the explosion site said that there were conflicting reports about the cause of the incident. People were hypothesizing about everything from a gas main burst to a Terrorist attack. The reporter continued by stating that Homeland Security and the FBI were immediately dispatched to Boston. The reporter stopped talking when the anchor, who is overly paid with bleached teeth, told the onsite reporter that the Mayor was making a statement. The camera cut away from the reporter and focused on the Mayor who was in a Boston College Golden Eagle sweatshirt. The Mayor stated the obvious about the explosion and added, "There will be hell to pay for this cowardly act by some radical Terrorist group!" Yet, without providing any additional details of the investigation, the Mayor seemed to speak in rhymes. Reese's attention drifted away from the Mayor's unpersuasive rhetoric as she imagined how worried she'd feel if Jim were alive and of how pissed he'd be about the station.

Her stomach growled, and Reese returned to reality. Reese decided to have a light dinner, take her medication, and call it a night to start fresh in the morning. Reese closed her eyes, and shortly thereafter she began to dream. It was a dream of her playing in the backyard as a little girl--playing by herself, having tea parties with her dolls, running, and jumping. And like other dreams Reese had every night, a faceless person came out of the woods, sat next to little Reese, and talked to her. Yet little Reese could never hear the words spoken. Frightened by the faceless person, little Reese would get up from the table and run to the house as fast as her little legs carried her, but little Reese ran in slow motion, and "no face" caught up to her, picked her up, and swallowed her whole---first the head---then torso---and her feet.

Reese's eye opened abruptly, and her body was soaking wet from sweating; she rose from the bed and looked at the clock on the stand which read 10:45pm. The headache was gone, and she felt fully refreshed. She got up from the bed and decided that she wanted to get out of the house for a while, so she went to the bathroom and turned on the shower. While the water heated, she went to her closet and pulled out some clothes to wear. She picked out her favorite outerwear which was a dark cashmere turtle neck, black form fitting jeans, and knee high boots. When she looked at the boots there was crusted mud under the soles. She put the boots back and chose another pair. She went into the bathroom and stepped into the shower. Fifteen minutes later she was looking in the mirror drying off. When she stopped, stared at herself, and muttered, "BITCHIN, with a capital B." Reese didn't wake up from her dream Rita did, and she was ready to hit the town, again....

Rita dressed and headed for the garage by way of her private entry way, so that she didn't have to bump into anyone. Rita crossed the rose garden and walked toward a building that resembled an aircraft hangar. There was a control panel on the side of the door, and Rita entered a code; the red light indicator turned green upon receiving the right code, and the huge doors begin to hiss softly. The door slowly opened revealing a collection of classic cars that would've made Howard Hughes feel like a welfare case. Reese's father took pride in collecting fine automobiles from all over the world. Rita walked through the massive museum and into another part of the garage where the everyday cars were kept. She passed a Chrysler 300 Sedan and made a reminder to take the vehicle back to the carpool tomorrow. Next to the Sedan was a true American tradition in muscle cars—the 1964 Pontiac GTO. Rita loved this car because of the 6.4 liter 389 cubic inch V8 with 325 horsepower. "It'll make guys my bitch in no time." Rita chuckled as she arrived at the storage box where the keys were kept and entered another code. The door opened, and Rita took out the keys for the GTO. Rita walked over to the manmade vibrator, opened the driver's side door, and got in. The plush leather interior was in its original condition with a high gloss shine. The leather was free of cracks and any signs of wear and tear. Rita started the beast with one turn of the key, and the monster came to life. Rita sat there for a minute listening to the hum of the V8; she put the car in drive and pulled out of the garage heading for her preordained meeting with a special someone---a person with close ties to a senator of the great state of Massachusetts. Rita planned to surprise the "special someone" who was clueless of Rita's intentions of bringing down that crazed bitch Mrs. Alice Clayton. Rita looked into the rear view, noticed that she had a sinister smirk on her face, and death on her mind.

CHAPTER EIGHT

John and Chyna reached the command post that was located a few yards from the bombing. It was a chaotic scene. John thought of movies and television reports of war throughout IRAQ and IRAN, but never would he have imagined such a scene here in Boston. Chyna rushed from John's side to help the injured. John continued to the tent where he spotted his commanding officer, Chief of Police, Robb St. Evans, loudly barking orders to someone on the phone, "I DON'T GIVE A FLYING FUCK, GENERAL! DO NOT BRING ANY TANKS OR NATIONAL GUARD INTO MY CITY! WAIT FOR MY PHONE CALL! IF I NEED YOU!" The six-foot seven behemoth of a man originated from the streets of

Boston and had one of the cleanest police records of crime in the country.

Since becoming Chief of Police, St. Evans's crime rate dipped to a staggering 25% over an 8 month time period and continued to plummet. The Mayor, who should have been proud of the fact that his city had one of the lowest crimes rates, hated the publicity the Chief received. The two public officials often bumped heads over budget cuts in the police department. The Mayor devilishly received some satisfaction from Jim's death after discovering that the Chief and Jim were cousins; the Mayor overheard a few guests talking at the Withers' estate during Jim and Reese's reception.

Knowing that his term was almost up, given the Chief's approval rating, and Jim's in-laws' connections, the

Mayor concluded that he'd lose the mayoral seat for certain. The Mayor didn't foresee receiving enough money to launch a good fight during his reelection campaign. The Mayor mischievously contrived a plan to become good friends with Chief St. Evans to win a reelection because he feared talks from his constituents of the Chief's serious consideration of running for the mayoral seat, and the Mayor meticulously twisted the fibers of his plan knowing that he would lose the race like throwing piss in the wind if it wasn't successful. So the Mayor gave the Chief breathing room, stayed in the background, and continued to give interviews to anyone with a camera and a mike.

John approached his boss cautiously and spoke, "Chief, how many are dead and how many hurt?" The Chief replied, "Miraculously, no one died. What you see here are a bunch of scrapes and bruises, broken windows, and debris from the blast." John looked at his superior with a stunned look.

Confused John asked, "How in the hell was that possible? Shit Robb! I felt that blast 8 or 9 blocks over. There should be bodies sprayed out all over the streets."

"Look John," the Chief's expression was that of a soldier about to go to war as he spoke to his most trusted officer. "This information I'm about to give you is for your ears only. Only a few high ranking officials actually know or have some clue of what happened." John listened. "About 5:00pm the Watch Commander received a package with your name on it and put it on your desk."

"A package? For me? From who?" John questioned. The Chief raised his hand to silence John, so he could finish. John stopped talking, and the Chief continued. "Someone must have thought that you'd be back after lunch, but you got the call for that homicide on State Street. Anyway, the package, as I was told, was sitting on your desk for a while until one of the officers became nosey and read what was on the card. The card read: 'Happy Anniversary John! Die like your partner Jim who now rots in hell!' And it was signed A.M.C." John was more confused than ever; he was unsure what to ask his boss with so many questions wandering through his head, but he read the Chief's face and chose to wait. Chief St. Evans glared around the room then continued his detailed explanation. "So the officer contacted the Watch, and then

I received the call, ordered for everyone to leave the building, and meet at the evacuation area. The bomb techs came in, scanned the package, and discovered a bomb with a cell phone timer relay attached to it. What you see here is a result of the bomb." John knowing that Chief St. Evans was done shouted, "What the fuck!!! Someone is trying to kill me now? And who in the hell is A.M.C?" Suspicion about Jim's death churned in John's head. "What the fuck?" John was literally lost for words. The Chief commanded, "I want you and that rookie to take the lead on this one and make it PRIORTY NUMBER ONE. If ANYBODY, I do mean ANYBODY tries to get in your way while conducting the investigation, call me day or night, and I'll fuck em' like an extra from "OZ." Nobody and I do mean nobody is going to shit on my grass and leave it for me to pick up." The Chief growled. With that John searched for Chyna to start on what might become the biggest case the city had ever known.

CHAPTER NINE

Rita drove past the wreckage she caused earlier in the day, and she realized that she probably used too much C4 to blow up the station, but she knew that it'd draw attention away from Tara's investigation. Rita thought that it was ingenious for her to write the initials A.M.C on the card hoping that some Matlock in the force would develop a lead to that maniacal bitch. And since it was the two year anniversary of Jim's death, Rita knew that the Police Station was a great idea because John would be quite tender.

Rita focused her attention on a new task; she was on her way to an upscale bar by the wharf because according to her sources Senator Richard Gregory Clayton's personal secretary, Denise Rodgers, was going to be there. The Senator was in town before the bombing because Congress was on a hiatus. Of course the Senator's personal secretary traveled with him, and she just happened to be young, gorgeous, 5'5, 140 lbs., and had a voluptuous figure. The source expected Denise to be with a group of girls enjoying the night on the town despite the ordeal with the bombing earlier.

Rita pulled up in front of the restaurant and pulled up to the Valets; the young guys were standing around looking bored when they heard the car and saw Rita getting out. They almost broke their necks running over each other. Rita smiled to herself and waited until the victorious one appeared in front of her. The kid looked to be 17 or 18. Out of breath and straightening his clothes he welcomed Rita to the restaurant and gave her a claim slip for the GTO. Rita demanded the young kid have her car standing by because she wouldn't be too long; then she handed the kid a hundred dollar bill. The kid took the money without looking at the denomination and slid it into his shirt breast pocket. He thanked Rita and got into the GTO. The kid slammed his foot on the accelerator and peeled off leaving dark tire tracks on the cement. The Valets looked at Rita thinking she was going to be pissed and request for management to complain, but instead she looked at them and said, "Driving it is almost better than sex," as she strut into the restaurant.

Rita stopped at the doorway, took in the atmosphere, and made a mental note to return to that restaurant to indulge in the cuisines. Rita waltzed over to the bar and asked the bartender for a Sam's. The bartender complied and gave her a bottle with a cold glass. Ignoring the frost mug Rita picked up the bottle and took a swig. Resting her back against the bar Rita noticed a group of men at the corner of it. Rita thought they were some college or high school buddies trying to pick up lonely women. One of the guys high-fived another guy and walked towards Rita, strutting as if he was on the Discovery Channel stalking his mate. The guy was dressed in a tasteful BROOKS BROTHERS suit and $1,600.00 loafers. He planted himself next to Rita, "Hi, my name is Chip." Rita was taking a sip of her beer when he said his name and spewed it out into the open area like she'd taken a hard hit to the stomach. Laughing Rita looked at Chip and said, "Get the fuck out of here! Seriously! Your name is CHIP?"

Chip snobbishly replied, "Yeah, so…?"

Rita chuckled, "Look Chipper, I'm not here to get picked up right now, and your advances need improvement, so I'm going to let you down real easy, so you can save face with the "SKULLS" over there. Turn around, walk back with your chest stuck out like you've conquered a small village, and lie about what I just told you. Okay?" Not waiting for a response Rita heard an overly boisterous sound of laughter coming from the corner of the restaurant and locked on to her target. Rita put down her beer and noticed that Chip was still there. Rita stared at him, kissed him on the mouth, and headed toward her mark. Rita heard the cheers from the "SKULLS" as Chip walked back to the pack like Leonidas from the "300," giving high fives and chest bumps.

While walking away Rita shook her head and smirked. Noticing her mark walk toward the women's restroom, Rita waited a few seconds and entered. Denise Rodgers aka the mark was at the mirror fixing her makeup and snorting something. Rita watched Denise out the corner of her eye and entered an empty stall. Looking through the crack, Rita took note of Denise's actions and clothing, then without hesitation Rita retrieved her smart phone and began to video tape Denise. Denise stood at the mirror and exhibited no concern that she had company in the restroom as she continued snorting cocaine. Rita thought, "Damn! This girl is snorting heavily." Denise finished up by gently rubbing her gums with coke and was checking her makeup when her cell phone rang. Denise grabbed her purse and rushed to find her phone; when she did retrieve it, she looked at it and smiled gleefully at the Caller ID. "Hi Daddy!" Denise addressed her lover. Rita listened intently and backed down a little since she assumed Denise was talking to her father. "I miss you Daddy. When are you going to come over to the hotel and take care of this kitty cat? It's purring for you baby." Rita perked up and put her ear completely on the crack of the stall. Then Denise's attitude quickly changed from playful to Damien. "WHAT THE FUCK DO YOU MEAN THAT YOU'RE NOT COMING OVER? LOOK SENATOR CLAYTON, WHY IN THE HELL DID YOU BRING ME TO BOSTON?" Denise stopped and listened. Judging by Denise's facial expression Rita could tell that Denise was fed up with the Senator and decided to play this for all it's worth. Denise continued her tirade,

"STAY WITH YOUR OLD CRUSTY ASS WIFE SENATOR BECAUSE YOUR MOUTH AND DICK ARE NO LONGER WELCOME TO PERUSE MY BODY!" Denise hung the phone up and threw it back into her purse. Denise, looking more upset, grabbed a silver pen-like container from her purse, put it up to her nose, and inhaled heavily. Rita, sensing that was her cue, flushed the toilet, opened the door, and headed towards the sink while Denise freshened her makeup. Rita looked at Denise through the mirror and attempted to console her by saying, "Girl, I don't mean to pry, but fuck him! You don't need that shit in your life." Denise, now crying, had mascara running down her cheeks. She sniffled, looked at Rita, and said, "I know. Fuck that old ass prick. The only reason I was fucking him was because he is the Majority

Leader of the Senate." Rita thought to herself that this woman could cause a whole lot of shit with Alice Clayton. Rita kept it cool and talked with Denise for a few more minutes. Denise finally invited Rita back to her suite at the Four Seasons Hotel. Rita agreed, and Denise gave her the spare key and told Rita that she'd meet her there in 20 minutes. Rita took the hotel key, kissed Denise on the lips, and left the restroom. Just to make sure that Denise wasn't trying to pull a fast one on her, Rita waited inconspicuously in the crowd and watched Denise at a table hugging and kissing her friends while telling them that she was leaving. And with that Rita headed for the entrance and for her car.

CHAPTER TEN

Senator Richard Gregory Clayton III was in his private study when he called Denise. He actually loved Denise not just for the sex, but he loved Denise because she didn't expect anything from him---not power, money, or gifts. She was a joy to be around. Richard had been married to Alice Marie for over two decades, and even though they both came from families with power and money, it was his wife who obnoxiously abused their status causing the Senator to stay in Washington for prolonged periods of time; he couldn't stand being around his wife. Alice was not very pleasant to be around. Since the Withers merger was unsuccessful, Alice was more power hungry than ever. Plus Alice had four plastic surgeries to her face, breast, and buttocks making her look like a failed contestant on HBO's "THE BUNNY RANCH."

Richard looked at his cell phone knowing that Denise was extremely upset. Richard wanted to spend time with her, but he had not been home in over two months, and he needed to be around the house for face time. Richard decided to let Denise cool off, and he hoped to make it up to her when they got back to Washington. But unbeknownst to Richard, Alice was listening to his conversation on the intercom in her private study, was writing down information about Denise, and contemplating how she would take care of the little whore. Alice drew a skull around Denise's name and pondered whether to call the Figure to take care of the tramp, or if she should let the whole scenario between Denise and her cheating ass husband play itself out. Alice slouched back into her chair enjoying the fact that she had the power to fuck up anybody's life if she willed it. Then a knock came at the door, and Alice's assistant walked in with papers for her to sign and notified her of the Senator's request for her company in the master bedroom. Alice nodded, took the papers away from her assistant, and began to sign them. When Alice finished, she got up from her desk and headed toward the master bedroom where her powerless husband the GREAT SENATOR OF MASSACHUSETTS awaited. Alice opened the massive door to the master bedroom and stepped in to discover her husband lying naked in the bed. The Senator thought he might as well play the role of loving husband at least until he went back to Washington. Alice looked at her husband and started to undress revealing her new breasts while leaving clothes in a trail behind her from the doorway to the bed. Alice thought she might as well play the role of loving wife until he went back to Washington. She continued to think about gutting that bitch ass assistant of his. When Alice got to the bed, she lifted the covers and got in. Mr. and Mrs. Clayton both looked at each other for what seemed to be minutes, turned their back on each other, and went to sleep.

CHAPTER ELEVEN

Rita arrived at 1:30 a.m. and pulled into an empty parking lot next to the Four Seasons. Rita didn't want to be seen coming and going into the hotel, so she went through the back of the Hotel where there was an open door. Rita assumed that the door was left open by smoking employees because she could see cigarette filters in the pottery. There wasn't much action. Rita found the freight elevator and took up it up to the 25 floor to the Executive's suites. When Rita located Denise's room, she swiped the key card, and the light on the panel didn't turn green. Rita slowly swiped the keycard again and waited for the light to turn green while thinking Denise had given her the wrong room number because she was high. Upset, Rita turned to walk away, when the door clinked, so Rita hurriedly pushed the handle down to gain access to the suite.

Rita looked over the spacious suite and began to search for incriminating information on the Senator. Rita went in the study where Denise's luggage was being kept and riffled through them with precision. Looking at her watch, Rita configured how long it would take Denise to get from the restaurant to the hotel. Rita estimated that she probably had a good 10-13 minutes left. Rita walked over to the desk; she opened files emblazoned with the Senate's stamp and began to look through them. After flipping through numerous files, Rita feared that she wouldn't find anything, but then she discovered something on the second to last page of a document that had a big red stamp which read: FOR YOUR EYES ONLY. Rita took out her phone and scanned the documents not knowing what Intel she was collecting until the name Withers Enterprises popped out at her. Rita wondered what the hell was going on and questioned why the Senate was targeting Reese's family. Rita continued reading through and scanning the papers. Then Rita whispered, "…investigations into the merger with Deutche Rail Works and Withers Enterprises and the names of …Holy shit! Claytons Rail, LLC owner Alice Marie Clayton is requesting the assistance of her husband's office to investigate the Withers…Son of a bitch." Then Rita heard the front door buzz, but it didn't open on the first try buying Rita enough time to shove all of the documents back into the file. Rita put the file back where she got it and rushed over to the couch awaiting Denise's entrance to the suite.

Denise stumbled into the suite looking dazed and confused. Denise looked at Rita pointing a finger and slurring, "I don't want to be disturbed, and if the Senator calls, wake me for the Senate Hearing." Rita smirked at Denise and thought, "Too much cocaine. Denise totally forgot who I am and that she gave me the key to her suite. She thinks that she's back in Washington, and I'm her assistant. WOW." Rita rose from the couch and followed Denise to the master bedroom where Denise fell over the bed and passed out. To make sure Denise was completely out, Rita went into a satchel and pulled put a white container of Chloral Hydrate aka Ethanol, and a cloth. Rita opened the top lid of the bottle, took the cloth, and dowsed it with Ethanol. Rita walked over to Denise, put the cloth over her nose, and covered her mouth making sure that Denise inhaled the fumes. Rita waited for a few minutes and laid Denise's head down; she checked Denise's pulse and the dilation of her pupils. Rita thought, "When Denise wakes up in the morning, she's going to have the headache of the God's." Rita went back to the study, continued reading, and scanning the inquiry into the Withers-Clayton merger.

After reading all the pages, Rita's anger for that bitch Alice Clayton climaxed to a new level. Looking at her watch, Rita noticed that it was almost 5am, and she had to rush home to awaken Reese. Rita put everything back where she found it minus any fingerprints or anything that would suggest that she was there. Rita left the Four Seasons and arrived home before the staff began their day. Rita rushed to the closet, opened the secret panel, quickly disrobed all her clothes, closed the secret door, checked to make sure nothing was out of place for nosey ass Reese, and when Rita was satisfied, she put on pajamas, got into bed, and fell asleep awakening Reese through the power of suggestion.

Minutes later Reese woke up feeling like a million bucks. The migraine was gone, and the sun was shining through the blinds; Reese stretched, hopped out of bed, grabbed her remote for the television, turned it on, and headed to the bathroom to begin her daily routine. To Reese it was a brand new day with new patients coming in, and a new day not to worry whether or not she was cracking up.

Reese arrived at work just before 9 am. She turned off all the alarms and headed for her office. Maria came in about 5 minutes after Reese. Maria put her things away and knocked on Reese's door. Reese looking up from her desk told Maria to come on in. "Good morning Dr. Withers. How are you feeling today?" Maria inquired. Reese looked at her new employee, told her that she was feeling a lot better, and thanked her for asking. Reese and Maria sat in the office and reviewed yesterday's occurrences with the killing of that poor young girl who got car jacked, and the police building that exploded later that afternoon. The chit chat transferred to the patients scheduled for the day and the new files Maria needed to prepare. Maria got up from her chair, "Would you like some coffee Dr. Withers?"

"Thank you. I would love some. Black please," responded Reese. As Maria left the office, she hesitated by the file cabinet to ensure that the sounding device was still positioned correctly and discreetly. Maria made the coffee and decided to check her ear plug to see if she could get good audio from Reese's office. After putting the invisible ear plug into her ear, Maria called out to Reese from the kitchen, even though it was unprofessional, but Maria had to make sure that she could hear the conversations from anywhere in the office. Shockingly Reese answered back making Maria feel like she was JANET BOND the poorer cousin of JAMES BOND from the hood. The coffee maker finished, and Maria poured some into Reese's cup and took it to her. After giving the cup to Reese, Maria asked if she would like the office door closed. Reese nodded, and Maria closed the door behind her.

Maria pulled out her smart phone and checked her messages. Some of the messages were from the NATIONAL REPORTER office about receipts that she hadn't turned in. Maria made a mental note to run by the paper later that day to get reimbursed for her expenses. The other message came from another source named "A FRIEND." Maria received $10,000.00 in cash a few days ago in exchange for some information on the Senator's Aide. That was the most money Maria ever received for less than an hour's work. It was easy for Maria; all she did was get in contact with one of the reporters from a tabloid in Washington, dropped the information off at a prearranged location, picked up an envelope, and opened it not sure what she'd find, but like "A FRIEND" said there was $10,000.00 in cash inside. Now Maria was curious about who "A FRIEND" was and tried to hide and get a picture of the person who picked up the info, but then Maria got a phone call from "A FRIEND" saying that if she ever wanted any more money that she'd better follow the rules and do what was asked of her. After that conversation, Maria now $10,000.00 richer took her money and went home. But what Maria didn't know was that a few of those one hundred dollar bills were marked with tracers, so "A FRIEND" could track her anywhere in the city within a 20 mile radius.

"A FRIEND" got the information from under the assigned space, looked inside the manila envelope, received all the information on the Senator's Aide, and on the Senator himself. "A FRIEND" satisfied with the information, left the site, got into a dark vehicle, opened a hand held PDA, turned it on, and automatically received a

signal from one of the bills. "A FRIEND" was very pleased

with today's technology and began to follow the signal.

CHAPTER TWELVE

The signal from the packet brought Rita to a middle class neighborhood, and at this time of night everybody was sleeping or up watching the Late Show. Rita studied the house where Maria lived and took notes on obvious things such as who would walk the dog at night and who came home late. Rita sensing that the area was clear of anybody nosing around got out of the car and walked along the side Maria's house. Rita noticed that Maria's house wasn't all that secured, and anybody with the skills could break in without leaving a trace. Rita assumed that Maria lived by herself from what she could tell by looking inside at the dishes in the sink, but Rita figured that she'd pinpoint her assumption after further investigation.

Rita left Maria's property and didn't look back; she got into her car and paused in the driver's seat looking over the area but noticed no movement. Rita started the car, kept the lights off, and drove down the road into the dark. After driving about 12 feet, Rita turned her lights on and wondered how she would handle Maria. A day ago Rita checked the internal messages from the secret office security system and discovered a live image of Maria in Reese's office placing devices behind the closet door and the file cabinet. There was also a section on the computer program for live audio from the elevator lobby. Rita clicked on the shortcut for that section and heard Maria's entire National Reporter call involving information on Mrs. Clayton and Reese. Rita transferred all the computer information into her personal file, erased Reese's file, and changed the time and date so that when Reese opened the file it would be empty.

After retrieving the messages, Rita became suspicious of Maria and whoever she was actually working for, and Rita questioned whether to consider Maria a friend or foe. After a thorough background check, Rita eventually concluded that Maria could be useful in helping bring down Mrs. Clayton and draw more of the heightened attention over the city's major crimes towards Mrs. Clayton. All of those discoveries and connections led Rita to the restaurant to meet Denise and to the discovery of the investigation into the Withers-Clayton failed merger.

Reese shouted, "Maria! Where are the files you were supposed to prepare and bring to me?" Maria quickly snapped out of her daydream, got up from her desk, and hurried into Reese's office to give her the prepped files and the patient roster for the day. The front lobby door opened, and the whimsical chime at the door rang. Maria excused herself to attend to the person in the lobby. Then Maria called Reese on the intercom to notify her of Ms. Lilly Thompson's arrival. To which Reese replied, "Good! Send her in." Reese stood up and waited for Lilly, who was a 35 year old nurse who as stated in her questioner suffered from a bipolar disorder and self-esteem issues. Reese shook her hand and guided Lilly to the couch, and Maria closed the door. No one noticed Rita standing in the mirror with her arms folded glaring at Maria then Rita's image slowly disappeared.

Back at the Clayton estate, Mrs. Alice Marie Clayton was sitting in the breakfast cabana wearing her white robe and stiletto shoes reading the morning paper when her husband walked in. Mr. Richard Gregory Clayton III walked over to his cosmetically altered wife and placed a kiss on her forehead; he could taste the Botox on his lips which made him gag, so he reached for a glass of orange juice to get the taste out of his mouth. Alice Marie put down the paper, closed her eyes, and lightly touched her husband's hand---she felt like retching her morning smoothie all over his prudish face. Richard lazily said, "Good Morning dear. How did you sleep?"

Alice Marie answered, "Slept quite well. I'm glad that you're home. I've missed your warm embrace at night." Alice Marie thought she was going straight to hell for that bullshit answer. "But at least it sounded genuine," she whispered. Richard knew that she was full of shit, yet he couldn't believe that she'd actually tried to sound compassionate. His mind wasn't on his MADE IN CHINA wife but on his lovely assistant Denise who was all alone at the Four Seasons. Richard knew he had to make up some excuse to get away from Alice. So Richard nonchalantly made polite conversation, "So what kind of plans do you have for today my love?"

"I'm meeting the girls today for lunch and doing some charity work at the Boston Girls and Boys Club. And you? What are you planning to do on your hiatus?" Alice Marie inquired. Richard figured his wife had just provided him with an excuse to sneak away to see Denise. "I'm planning to go downtown to check on the progress of the bombing and do some photo ops with the rescue workers. It'll look good for the upcoming elections."

Alice Marie frowned at her husband knowing damn well that he was going downtown to fuck his mistress, so she scowled, "Maybe I should go with you. It'll be good publicity for the family." Sensing that he just fucked up he mentioned that he'd probably be in meetings with the Mayor and the Chief of Police after the tour of the site. Alice Marie knew full well not to argue with her husband, so she let it slid and reminded herself to get in contact with her contractor to give the order to exterminate Denise before she left Boston. Alice Marie said, "Okay love, just be careful and remember we have dinner plans with the Stevenson's at the club at 7pm." Richard grimaced and with an open hand smacked himself against the forehead, "Damn, honey I forgot. I'll be there." He got up from the table and strolled over to give his wife a kiss on the lips, and for a moment, just a brief moment, he swore that he tasted embalming fluid. He gagged and quickly left to get dressed, so that he could bust a quickie with Denise at the Four Seasons. "Mental note," he thought, "Don't forget to take the Cialis this time."

Mrs. Clayton looking away from her paper looked at her husband as he walked away thinking to herself, "If he wasn't the third most powerful man in America, I would have his intestines ripped from his gut and have it fed to the neighbor's dog. What a wonderful thought!" After the investigations into the Withers, she would have to put in a special call to make her husband's death a national Memorial Day. Alice Marie knew that she would have to shop for a special dress for his funeral. "Damn, it's going to be a beautiful funeral." She said out loud as she picked up her coffee cup and peered out the window

admiring the estate grounds.

CHAPTER THIRTEEN

As John and Chyna left the bombing area, John was still in a lurch. He worried that someone was trying to kill him and that whoever it was could've killed Jim a few years ago. Chyna sensed that something agitated John, but he hadn't said anything about it. Chyna couldn't take the silence any longer, "God damn it John! What the fuck is going on! You haven't said jack shit to me since we left the bombing site. Are you planning to tell me what the fuck is going on, or do I have to sit here and question why in the hell I ever moved from New York?" Chyna abruptly ejected. John hadn't heard a word she said; he glanced at her then back at the road. "JOHN, STOP THE FUCKING CAR!!!!" Chyna screamed with terror. John snapped out of the trance just in time to put on the brake with the force of

God to prevent them from plowing into a stopped 18' wheeler. "Oh fuck, what the...wholly shit..."sputtered John now drenched in sweat.

"Are you okay John?" Chyna inquired. John regaining his senses looked over to Chyna and nodded, and then he pulled his car over to the side of the road and parked. Staring at the steering wheel John broke his silence and said, "The bombing may have not been a terrorist act. It may have been a plot to kill me." Chyna froze and looked at her partner as if he had flipped his lid. "What the hell are you talking about? Who's trying to kill you, and why blow up a fucking building just to get to *you*?" John told Chyna what the Chief revealed to him about the package, the initials left on the package, and his assumptions that his former partner's death may not have been an accident. Chyna now looking out the passenger side window said, "Shit!"

John said they would have to go to the police impound and locate Jim's car. Normally the police impound would sell all abandoned or usable vehicles to scrap yards, but John wanted to check anyway, despite Jim's car being a charcoaled brick. John reached for his phone, placed a call to the police impound, and asked to speak to the person in charge. John gave his name and rank hoping for a faster search than a normal person would receive just calling in for a towed vehicle. John finally reached Sergeant Taylor who was in charge of the police impounds. John announced, "Sergeant. This is Lead Detective John Campbell. I have an unusual request to ask of you."

"Sure Detective. I'll try to assist you in whatever way I can…what's up?" replied Taylor.

"Do you still happen to have Police Captain Jim Henry's vehicle on the lot?"

"Damn Detective! That was over two years ago. I'll have to check, but normally when a case is closed we scrap it," said Taylor.

"I know, I know, but could you just check for me and call me back at this number a.s.a.p.?" John pleaded.

"Sure thing! I'll get on it right now, but don't expect any gold on the other side of the rainbow Detective." Taylor responded.

"Copy that! I'll be waiting for your call," John said and hung up the phone.

John knew it was a shot in the dark, but he had to try. Chyna looked at John and asked, "What about that homicide on State Street?" John had forgotten all about it. "Don't you think that it's damn peculiar for someone to kill a woman and carjack a piece of shit car in the middle of the afternoon on one of Boston's busiest streets?"

John looking ahead said, "What's your point Chyna?"

Chyna shaking her head said, "Follow me on this. Someone killed a woman and dumped her body in the middle of the street. Then they took a bullshit compact Ford Fiesta. Who's dying to buy one of those on the black market? And who would need or pay for the parts off it?"

"Ok, I'm with you so far," added John.

Chyna continued, "And weren't we supposed to return to the station to turn in our paperwork from that anonymous call about a suspicious person lurking around the Hancock building garage after lunch when we got the call?"

John solemnly replied, "Shit, we were supposed to be IN that building." Chyna raised her hand to signal John to let her finish. "We were only at the scene what…a good 15 minutes or so? Then the bomb went off?"

John said, "You think that the death of that girl and the bombing are connected somehow?" Chyna looked at her partner with one of those "WHAT THE FUCK DO YOU THINK?" kinds of looks. John thought about what Chyna said and concluded that someone had to be a cold motherfucker to kill someone and disguise it by blowing up a fucking Boston police building. John told Chyna to call the morgue to check on the identification of the victim, and then something else popped into John's mind---Reese. He hadn't spoken to Reese since Jim's funeral. He considered stopping by her office, if she still practiced, to check on her.

Chyna ended the phone call and looked down at her notes; she told John, "The victim's name was Tara Meyers, age 25, from somewhere down south, but her most recent address was in Revere. She's single, no kids, had about $50.00 on her, and a couple of pre-paid credit cards in her wallet." Chyna continued to go through her notes and said, "Tara worked for a catering outfit in Salem for about 3 years called "Forever More Catering," and there was a business card on her that the Dr. Kim thought was kind of odd and out of place. It was the business card of a Mrs. Alice M. Clayton."

John looked at his partner, "The Socialite…the wife of Senator Richard Clayton III?"

"Yep," replied Chyna. John turned on the sirens, whipped the car around, and headed for the Boston's Morgue. "What's up?" Chyna shouted while desperately trying to put on her seatbelt.

"I have a fucking hunch about your little conspiracy, Agent Scully." Then the phone rang. John looked down at the caller id and answered it, "Lead Detective Campbell." Listening to the other side John had an instant burst of energy. "YOU'RE SHITTING ME! YOU STILL HAVE THE CAR! PULL IT AND I WANT

THE FULL WORK UP ON IT! CHECK EVERYTHING! THE BRAKES, THE STEERING COLUMN, EVERYTHING…NO ONE GOES HOME AND THIS IS COMING STRAIGHT FROM THE CHIEF!!!!" John hung up the phone and smiled to himself, but he also prayed that his friend actually died from the ice and not from someone's dirty handiwork.

CHAPTER FOURTEEN

Reese finished up her last patient for the day at 4:15pm and sat back exhausted. She did well her second day back to work. She'd treated a total of 6 patients, and according to Maria another 6-8 patients were scheduled for tomorrow. Maria called back on the intercom, "Lead Detective John Campbell is on line one. You want to take it?" Reese hadn't heard that name since Jim's funeral; she pushed the button to connect the call, "John hello dear! How are you?" Reese tried to sound cheerful. John sensed uneasiness in Reese's voice, and he began to regret the phone call, "Hey love. I'm fine. I'm so sorry that I haven't been keeping in touch. Work has just been so busy…especially now that I'm following some leads on the bombing."

"That's okay because I myself just started back to work yesterday." Reese answered.

"Would you like to meet for dinner…just to catch up on things?" Reese reluctantly agreed. So John replied, "Meet me at that new restaurant. You know the one that's down by the wharf at about 8:30 pm. Is that ok?" Reese ejected an unenthusiastic, "Sure," before hanging up the phone. Then Maria walked in asking Reese if she needed anything else before she left because the patient roster and preliminary paperwork was done for tomorrow. Reese thanked Maria and told her that she could leave, and she'd see her bright and early tomorrow. Maria left locking the lobby office behind her and headed for the elevators. Maria reached inside her purse to grab her cell phone to call her boss at the National Reporter. Maria's boss answered, and

Maria told him that she would be coming in to give him a progress report. The elevator doors opened, and Maria walked in forgetting that the audio and video cameras were taping her every word.

Meanwhile John and Chyna arrived at the Morgue. "Do you think it's wise to tell Monica Withers that her husband was probably murdered even though we haven't completed a thorough investigation of the new evidence?" Chyna asked. John exited the car without a response, walked over, and opened the door for his partner, "I'm not going to tell her anything yet---not until I know for sure what happened to Jim." They walked past the receptionist's desk and into the M.E.'s office where Dr. Kim was eating a bologna sandwich while peering at a computer screen on his desk. Tara's body lay on the table behind him with her chest cracked open revealing Hannibal Lector's Thanksgiving feast including her delectable brain left exposed from the huge gun blast.

John approached Dr. Kim regarding the flimsy lettuce and mustard dripping from his sandwich, "Damn Kim, how in the hell can you eat around a fucking dead person?" Chyna nauseatingly glared at Tara's body on the table then turned and left the room without saying anything. "Shit a person's got to eat. You want some?" Kim held the sandwich up to John's mouth, but John waved it off. "Where are the victim's belongings?" John inquired. Kim pointed towards the other metal table where a plastic bag contained all of Tara's possessions. John examined the contents and asked, "Have you completed your autopsy?"

"Her death was instantaneous. She never knew what hit her," ejected Dr. Kim. John discovered business cards in Tara's wallet for her job and the mysterious business card of the one and only Mrs. Alice Marie Clayton. John turned the card over on the back and discovered that there was another number on it. John's brain kicked into high gear. He took the business cards and signed for them leaving the other property behind, and as he left he told Kim to keep him informed if anything else came up. Kim not looking up from his computer just raised his hand acknowledging John. John entered the hallway where Chyna was sitting on a bench drinking water. "You okay?" John asked as he bent down to console the rookie detective. Chyna looked up and said, "Yeah, but how in the hell can a man eat a freaking sandwich with a dead body less than 5 feet from him?"

John didn't answer. All he did was shake his head.

John and Chyna left the City Morgue. John looking at his watch told Chyna that he had to drop her off at the Commend Tent so he could meet with Monica. John instructed Chyna to investigate Tara's responsibilities at the catering business and all of her recent clients. Chyna looked at John in annoyance of his orders, "He acts as if this is my first investigation," she thought. John didn't tell Chyna that he planned to check out Mrs. Alice Marie Clayton by himself. When they arrived at the Command Tent which was set up because of the bombing, Chyna got out and proceeded to the check point. Staying long enough to make sure she made it through the crowd, John left the area and headed to the restaurant to meet with Monica.

John made it to the restaurant where he parked his own car because he didn't trust the valets. Just as John crossed the parking lot he spotted an AUDI R8 GT driving up to the valet. John said, "SHIT that's a nice ass car." John enthusiastically waited to see who would emerge from the driver's side door as a valet rushed to open it. First, John saw two lusciously long legs appear from the car then his eyes perused the figure upward from the firm middle to the gorgeous face. John realized that those legs and that gorgeous ass body belonged to Reese. John pulled his hard on under control and called out to Reese as she was being handed a tag for her car. Reese turned around to see who was calling her name, and she spotted John walking up to her. Reese waved and smiled as John approached with his arms out stretched. They embraced each other and patted each other on the back. The embrace lasted longer than it was supposed to, but it didn't matter. John let Reese go and looked her up and down, "Damn Reese, you look fantastic." John continued to admire her figure as they walked toward the restaurant entrance.

"You look good too John. I see that Police work has been kind to you," Reese said giving him the once over. Reese was impressed; John looked good in his French cut suit. Reese admired John's decision to dress like a respectable banker or a stock broker not the usual off-the-rack Police officer. They held each other's hands and were about to enter the restaurant when one of the valet guys walked passed Reese to open the door. The boy glanced at Reese and paused, "Welcome Back."

Reese startled by his response said, "Excuse me?"

The Valet equally confused replied, "Welcome Back…from last night…remember?"

Reese looked at John then back at the Valet, "I'm sorry, but this is my first time here. You have me mistaken with another customer."

The valet was embarrassed, "I'm sorry, you look familiar. Gosh, there's a strong resemblance between you and a customer we had last night."

Reese answered, "That's okay I get that sometimes"

The valet looked at the AUDI R8 GT, "Is that your car?"

"Yes, not that it's any of your business. Why do you want to know?"

Admiring the R8 GT the valet said, "The customer who came in last night drove a 1964 GTO…another power automobile. I apologize for the confusion. Please enjoy your evening ma'am." Reese was puzzled and thought it ironic that her father owned a 1964 GTO, but she didn't say anything. John escorted Reese into the restaurant then he asked her if she wanted to have a drink at the bar while they waited for a table. Reese nodded, but she was preoccupied with the valet's comments. Reese wanted to review the security footage at the estate when she returned home to see if anyone had taken the car out last night.

After a few drinks their table was ready, and John and Reese enjoyed dinner while conversing about the past two years. Reese revealed to John that at the time of Jim's death she was pregnant, but that she'd miscarried. John sympathized with Reese and was pissed off at himself for not having kept in contact with her after Jim's passing. John reached out to touch Reese's hand, "I'm so sorry, and I promise that I'll do anything in my power to stay in contact with you." Reese patted his hand and gave John a smile then took a sip of water. John's cell phone rang. Startled, John grabbed his cell off his belt clip and answered abruptly, "Lead Detective Campbell?" He listened on the other end of the line to Sergeant Taylor who was overseeing the search detail on Jim's car. John's eyes widened and he couldn't hide the expression from

Reese. Reese mouthed the words, "What's wrong?" John read her lips and intently listened to Sergeant Taylor as he mouthed the words "Nothing," while shaking his head. John ended the phone call and nervously put his phone on his belt. "I need to go. That was an important lead into a critical investigation. I apologize love. I've enjoyed spending the evening with you catching up, and I've thoroughly appreciated the view." Reese blushed, yet she understood. John motioned the waiter for the check, but when it arrived Reese quickly handed over her credit card, and the waiter dashed off before John could stop him. Reese chuckled, "I got this John, but you'll get the next one okay?" John nodded and said, "You got it lady. I'm sorry I got to go. I'll call you." John reached over and kissed Reese on the cheek, pulled away, and looked at her with what might have been more than platonic affection. John turned and left the restaurant leaving Reese behind. Reese wasn't ready to go home yet, so she sat back down and waved for the waiter to bring her a slice of Tiramisu and coffee.

John's hurried walk became an outright 40 yard dash for his car. He got in, turned on the sirens, and screeched out of the parking lot leaving patrons and everyone in awe. John called Chyna and told her to get her ass to the police garage ASAP and that he was en route. John's blood pressure skyrocketed after hearing the news from the investigator. It was difficult to hide it from Reese since she was a trained psychiatrist.

John reached the garage, parallel parked, and rushed in to find Sergeant Taylor. John flashed his badge at the person at the front desk and asked to be directed to Taylor. Chyna arrived almost simultaneously and came in looking distraught, "John what the hell is going on?" John not paying attention to Chyna saw a short Spanish man in coveralls walking toward the both them. The Spanish man reached out his hand, and John shook it. "Detective Campbell I presume?" John nodded. "I'm lead investigator Sanchez. Sergeant Taylor asked me to walk you through my investigation. Let me start by saying that your partner's death was not an accident. He was murdered." John felt sick to his stomach and tried to speak but couldn't find the words. Chyna spoke for him, "Sanchez, how did you come to that conclusion. I mean it's been over two years for Pete's sake." Sanchez continued his report, "The original conclusion was that Jim lost control of his car during a snow storm, and given the weather conditions the CSIs didn't have any evidence that would've caused them to determine that there was foul play. Since John's request to reopen the case, we went back out to the scene and completed a more intense search of the site and car. We found no tire marks on the road before Jim's car veered off the cliff…and…we've noticed that the brake line was cut. I'm assuming that whoever conducted the first investigation believed that it was an accident and didn't bother to meticulously examine the charred pieces."

John, now more composed, looked at Sanchez, "I want a complete analysis and written report of the car tonight, if overtime is an issue tell them it's coming straight from the Chief." Sanchez felt nothing but remorse for John because he knew how close Jim was to him. "No problem John. I'll take care of it. If anything else comes up I'll call you. Sorry man." Sanchez said as he patted John on the shoulder.

John and Chyna walked out of the garage and stood on the steps. John reached for his phone to call the Chief. The Chief answered, and John told him about the new information. John's tone was so passionate that the Chief instructed him to go home immediately and clear his mind because he needed to flawlessly handle the investigation to find Jim's killer.

"It's now official. The Boston Police Department is about to hunt down a COP KILLER. My sole mission in life is to KILL WHO EVER MURDERED MY PARTNER." John contemplated.

CHAPTER FIFTEEN

When Reese made it home from her night out with John, she had to tell herself to excuse the sorted feelings she thought she had when they hugged, yet her mind continued to replay the conversations they had at dinner. Reese knew that there could never be a relationship with her dead husband's partner and best friend. But Reese's feelings were mixed, and she tried to forget John until a voice whispered, "Reese. There's nothing wrong with you opening your heart and finding true love again. It's ok if you find that cop attractive." Reese looking in the rear view mirror noticed that her image was replaced by Rita. Reese knew she had not taken her medication, yet she didn't panic. She spoke to Rita in a condescending voice.

"Look Rita, you know full well that I can't possibly feel anything for John. He is Jim's partner and best friend for God's sake." Rita asked with a smirk on her face, "Where is it written that you can't date your ex-husband's friend. Jim's dead honey and he's not coming back. Besides, he was an asshole anyway." Reese shook her head denying that her conscious, her sanity was betraying her. Rita glared at Reese, "I can read your thoughts dumb ass! You MUST believe that I'll never betray you…you can take that to the bank." Reese's thoughts drifted back to dinner, the hug John gave her, the intoxicating smell of his cologne, and the softness of his skin. It all made Reese feel secure and warm for the first time in many years. Rita added her two cents into the thought, "Yeah and the pussy is drying up like the Nevada desert! You got to do something fast OR I will." Reese could feel herself blush over Rita's comment. Then it hit Reese, so she asked, "What do you mean by OR I WILL?" Reese waited for an answer but there wasn't a reply. Reese looked into the rearview mirror hoping to see Rita, but it was just her face peering back at her. "I really need to up my dosages. I'm cracking the hell up." Reese said as she entered through the estate's gates. Reese drove toward the security building to check the surveillance tapes to see if anybody had taken her father's GTO.

    Reese pulled into her parking space, grabbed her belongings, and entered the office to look at the tapes. As Reese was about to review the tapes from the previous night, her cell phone rang; she looked at the screen and read "unknown caller." "Hello?"

"Reese? This is John." Reese was excited, but she tried not to give a hint of it in her reply. "Hello John. I would like to thank you for inviting me to dinner even though you didn't finish." She laughed. That queasy feeling began in Reese's stomach again.

"Look I'm so sorry about that and I would like to make it up to you. May I try again tomorrow night…if you know…if you're available?"

Reese sat in a revolving chair with her back to the monitor completely forgetting about the images on the video of the night before. The video displayed images of Rita pulling out of the garage in Reese's father's GTO. "I would love that John; yes I would love that very much," she paused and added, "John, you do understand that this isn't a date, right?"

John felt like he just got shot down over the Pacific by a freakin' F-15 fighter jet. "No…no of course Reese. I understand. I'll even pay this time. Can I call you later?" he asked.

"Yes. Please do call me when you get off John. I would love to finish our conversation from dinner." Reese hung up the phone and got up from her seat. She froze perplexed by her presence in the security office. "Ugh! For the life of me I can't remember why I came in here. Oh well." Reese gathered her things and headed toward the house to bathe and take her meds.

Reese made it to her bedroom where she put her things on the desk, turned on the television but muted the sound, walked over to the wet bar, and made herself a Dirty Martini. She took off her clothes, sent them down the laundry chute, and walked into the bathroom to shower. Reese stared in the mirror and again tried to ascertain why in the hell she went to the garage office. Still…NOTHING. So, Reese walked over to her nightstand, grabbed her medicine bottle, poured two tablets into the palm of her hand, put them in her mouth, and took a nice swig of the martini. One twenty minute shower later a drowsy Reese dried herself and lotioned her body. She took one more swig of the drink and got into bed where it didn't take long for her to fall right to sleep.

CHAPTER SIXTEEN

The Senator told his driver to pull over at the flower shop to pick up some roses for Denise. He tried reaching her since he'd left the estate, but Denise's phone went straight to voicemail. The Senator concluded that Denise was either still pissed off since he couldn't spend time with her and ignoring him or was sleeping late, but he didn't give a shit either way because he knew that Denise was a good fuck and that she loved doing things for him. He reminisced about receiving a blowjob from Denise under his desk during a Budget Session that lasted almost two hours. "Shit," the Senator thought while fondling his balls. "I must have come at least three times." The Senator chuckled at the thought because everybody in the room wondered where that thumping noise was coming from.

The driver pulled over at a flower boutique and opened the door for the Senator. Normally the Senator would have security with him, but he decided against it to be discreet. As the Senator entered the Flower Shoppe he noticed a stout lady who looked like she'd leaped fresh off the bottle of Mrs. Butterworth standing behind the counter. With a welcoming smile she stated, "Good Afternoon! How can I help you today?" The Senator cordially requested two dozen long stem sterling roses from Mrs. Butterworth, and he asked that they be wrapped together to make at a massive bouquet. Mrs. Butterworth, seeing dollar signs, jumped at the chance to up sale everything in the store, but the Senator frugally stated that his only purchase would be the roses.

When Mrs. Butterworth finished wrapping the roses, she rang his purchase up at the register. "Your total comes to $350.95. Will that be cash or credit?" As the Senator reached for his wallet he said, "That will be cash." Then he removed four crisp one hundred dollar bills and handed them over. Mrs. Butterworth attempted to make small talk, "She must be one lucky lady to receive such beautiful roses."

"Yes. Yes she is," the Senator replied as he stretched out his hand for his change urging Ms. Florida Evans to move her fat ass, so he could get out there. Sensing the tension, the woman slapped the change into the Senator's hand. The Senator shoved the money into his pocket, collected his purchase, and headed out the door. Mrs. Butterworth walked up to the door and peered through glass window admiring the Senator's chauffeured limousine. Unfortunately, she overheard the negativity spewing out of the Senator's mouth about her weight; it pissed her off. The Senator glanced back at the Flower Shoppe door and noticed that Mrs. Butterworth was looking at him waving her middle finger in the air. The Senator not to be out done flipped up both of his middle fingers at Mrs. Butterworth, and for good measure he stuck out his tongue as the Limo moved away from the curb, "Fucking peasants," the Senator said to himself. "Ah…now to the Four Seasons Hotel."

When they arrived, he told his driver to go around to the Service area, so he could inconspicuously slip in without being noticed by the media or any of his constituents. The driver obeyed and went around to the back; not waiting for the driver to completely stop the limo, the Senator picked up the flowers and hurried into the service entrance. Scampering through the hall and using the roses as face cover each time he passed under a security camera the Senator reached the elevators and pushed the penthouse button.

Arriving on the penthouse floor, the Senator exited the elevator and headed for Denise's room. Once he arrived he thought about knocking but quickly gave up on that notion because he was paying the bill. He grabbed the card key from his wallet and slid it through the slot, but nothing happened, so he slid the card again. The Senator cautiously entered the room hoping to discover his lover alone, but he anticipated her revengefully fucking another man. His temper was fuming with images of his sexy ass assistant with her legs spread open with some fucking geek in between them plowing for gold in THAR DARN HILLS, so the Senator dropped the roses on the floor and burst into the master bedroom like SWAT to catch them in the act, but to his amazement there was no geek or any man on top of his assistant just her…sleeping. Relieved, the Senator looked around for anything that resembled that a man had been there, but he couldn't find any evidence. Looking at Denise the Senator found renewed love for her. He walked over to the bed and sat beside her. He removed the comforter to reveal her voluptuous breasts then bent down to kiss one of her nipples as he did he realized that her breast was cold, damn cold. He ran his finger across Denise's deathly cold body then put two forefingers to her throat to feel for a pulse. "AW, SHIT,

SHIT, SHIT!" The Senator screamed out. "What the fuck did you do?" The Senator saw dried blood coming out of Denise's nostrils; he continued to curse when his brain kicked into self preservation mode. He got up from the bed, walked over to the window, withdrew his cell phone from his jacket pocket, and called for discreet help--- a cleaner of some sort to clean the shit up.

While waiting for the cleaners, the Senator collected all of the legislative papers and other important documents. The Senator came across a file stamped "TOP SECRET." As he read the information, he discovered that his wife was using his name to get a congressional hearing over some bullshit failed business deal. Then the Senator looked at Denise with the utmost hatred, "Did you and my wife have something going on behind my back? What the fuck is Alice up to?" KNOCK! KNOCK! The Senator gathered all the paperwork and carried them to the door. He opened the door where stood five tall, burly men in white coveralls and his driver. He let them in, described what he found, and instructed them to take care of it. The Senator immediately exited because he didn't want to know what they were going to do with Denise. He headed down the hall with his driver and got onto the elevator. Without exchanging glances the Senator stated, "My wife is getting way out of control. She needs to be taught a lesson. When the cleaners finish here, instruct them to make it look like an accident...like that cop a few years back. But wait until Congress is back in session." The driver acknowledged his orders, and they rode the elevator in silence.

CHAPTER SEVENTEEN

Mrs. Alice Marie Clayton, the daughter of the second most famous family next to the Kennedys, sat idly by in a modest Ford Lincoln Town car in a parking lot facing the service entrance to the Four Seasons Hotel waiting for her husband to reappear. Suddenly there was a lot of commotion after a white utility van pulled up, and five guys dressed in white coveralls jumped out and entered the hotel while the sixth guy waited with the motor running.

After over-hearing the conversation between her husband and his aide the night before, Mrs. Clayton decided to follow him today. She'd been at his first stop to the Florist Shoppe and tailed him to the Four Seasons, and she suspected that he and his mistress were somehow involved in the commotion. Then Senator Clayton appeared from the hotel service entrance with his driver, got into the limo, and screeched off. Mrs. Clayton decided to investigate the situation, so she waited what seemed to be an eternity; then the 5 men exited the hotel carrying a securely wrapped buddle. She wanted to get a closer look at the item they were carrying, so she decided to boldly approach the men as they shoved the bundle into the van. Without hesitation she announced, "Do you know who I am? I am Mrs. Richard Gregory Clayton III."

The tallest guy, probably the leader, frantically looked at Mrs. Clayton wishing that he'd never answered the phone for this gig. "I know who you are Mrs. Clayton, and unfortunately we can't discuss anything with you or show you what's inside the bundle. Frankly, it's none of your concern."

"Who in the fuck does your prick ass garbage smelling butt think you are talking to? Mrs. Clayton was irritated by this reject from hillbilly farms. "Let me explain something to you…you dumb mother fucker. You're carrying what appears to be a dead body in the middle of the day, and my husband walked out before you did, so he probably had something to do with it. Now, if I don't get a peek of what's inside that bundle of fucking joy your carrying, I'm going to call the police and have all your prissy asses arrested." The guys contemplated their next move, and Mrs. Clayton could hear nothing but curse words from everyone. Mrs. Clayton smirked at the degenerates and gave them something else to think about.

"What is my husband paying you for disposing of this bitch?"

"$3500.00," replied one of them.

Mrs. Clayton asked, "A piece?"

"No ma'am…for the whole job."

Mrs. Clayton sensing an opportunity suggested, "I'll give you boys $5,000.00 each for finishing this job, but I need to take a look at the body, and I would like for you gentlemen to do something else for me. I'll give you an extra…$10,000.00 each for a future job. Now I won't tell my husband about our agreement if you won't, and the money is yours. If you don't accept my terms then I'll put in an anonymous call to my husband." Mrs. Clayton took out her camera phone and started taking pictures of the crew and the wrapped bundle. "There! You morons were just caught disposing of a body. Question is…what will my husband do to you if he gets a phone call and those pictures?" The crew huddled to discuss their options and seeing that there weren't any they agreed to take the extra money from Mrs. Clayton. Then they reluctantly walked to the back of the van and proceeded to undo the top of the bundle exposing the deceased aide of the great Senator of Massachusetts. Mrs. Clayton stared down at the corpse, "You see bitch. No dick is worth dying over especially not another woman's dick. Rest in hell fish bait."

Mrs. Clayton bent down and gave the corpse a passionate kiss on the lips. The crew gaped in disgust and whispered, "What kind of crazy as shit is this? This woman is one ice cold bitch."

Straightening up, Mrs. Clayton demanded, "Everyone give me your licenses and phone numbers." The crew pulled their licenses out and began to write their information down when Mrs. Clayton's demeanor further deteriorated; her voice became so evil that the Devil had to make sure that he wasn't talking to himself. Mrs. Clayton glared at each member of her crew, "And if one of you, just one of you fuck me over I swear to you that not only will I fuck you in ways you can't even comprehend, but your family will suffer the same ultimate fate. I have the money and I have the power. I'll have you bitches selling tampons at the flea market after I'm done with you." By the look in their eyes Mrs. Clayton knew that her message was clear, so she pulled a wad of cash from her purse, peeled off the wrap around freshly minted one hundred dollar bills, and gave it to her lackeys. "Where are you taking her?" Mrs. Clayton asked.

"We're taking her to the marshes and burying her there."

"Good. Here's my private number. When you bury her, take a picture and send it to me. I want it for my scrap book." Mrs. Clayton instructed. They nodded in compliance then one of them took the number from her, and put it on the dashboard. Mrs. Clayton walked up to the leader of the crew and whispered in his ear, "When you get done with this job, get cleaned up and call me." Mrs. Clayton's hand found its way to his crouch and proceeded to caress his bulge. He felt ill but didn't dare say no to his new employer, so he muttered, "Yes ma'am," and gulped for air. Mrs. Clayton relishing in her power, kissed him on the cheek, and cried out as she walked away a cheerful, "TOODLES!"

Mrs. Clayton got back into her car, started the engine, and put the car into reverse but paused; she put the car back into park and sat for a moment to watch her very own KEEBLER elves hurriedly work. Mrs. Clayton could see that the leader was trying to control the situation and calm the guys down, but when that didn't work she saw the leader raise his hand and SMACK. The echo from the leader's back hand which landed squarely on the guy's cheek sounded as if he was a bitch who short changed a pimp. Mrs. Clayton became so aroused that she spread her legs open and pleasured herself in the parking lot.

The men competently completed their work, jumped into the van, and sped off. Watching the van take off, Mrs. Clayton wiped herself with a moist toilette, rolled down her window, and tossed it. Her next move was to head downtown to surprise her cheating, murderous husband at the bombing site. As Mrs. Clayton sped toward downtown, she pushed a button on her steering wheel and a computerized voice asked, "What number would you like to dial?" Mrs. Clayton answered, "Dial Figure." The voiced ceased, and the number tones were heard through the car speakers. The voice came on, "Dialing, please wait…" Mrs. Clayton's mood started to change from gitty to bitchy in a matter of seconds. The Figure's voice mail came on suggesting the caller leave a number and a message. Mrs. Clayton was pissed. "Why is it that every time I call you, you never pick up the god damn phone? I want you to call me back as soon as possible. We HAVE to meet. And I don't give a flying fuck about you not liking meeting face to face! Tough shit! CALL ME BACK!!!" She yelled out then disconnected the call. "God Damn Slackers," she said to herself as she entered the freeway and increased her speed.

CHAPTER EIGHTEEN

John contemplated the ludicrous possibility of someone trying to kill him. After learning that Jim's death wasn't accidental, John became enraged and had vivid visions of revenge. "Does the State street homicide have anything to do with the bombing at the station? And why would someone attack the station two years after Jim's death if the two incidents are connected? Damn," John thought, "Chyna was probably right. Who would be so damn cold to kill a woman in broad daylight and minutes later destroy a fucking police building? That's a cold son of a bitch. And how the fuck is Senator Clayton's wife involved?"

Amidst the chaotic thoughts clouding John's mind Reese's face appeared making John smile. He reminisced about the dinner they had the previous night. He thought about Reese's sexy physique blossoming from the car, the way she smelled, their kiss, and her supple skin. John knew deep down that he couldn't have romantic feelings for his partner's wife, but he just couldn't stop thinking about her. Especially, after the last conversation he had with her the night before. John caught himself in the mirror grinning until his cell phone vibrated startling him. He reached for his belt clip and answered his phone. It was the Chief, and he wanted John and Chyna to hurry back to the bombing site as soon as possible. John hung the phone up and pushed a pre-set number to call his partner.

John arrived at the scene and marveled at the site where the Boston police department building once stood. John pulled out his badge to show the patrolman standing guard at the entrance who kept the media and civilians at bay. The cleanup was already taking place, and as John approached the command tent, he could see that there were a lot of people talking with the Chief. John went inside quietly; he wanted to observe the scene and players before speaking, so he stood in the corner near the coffee and donuts listening to various conversations until he heard a slightly familiar voice pulling him in its direction. The Chief was talking to Senator Clayton and the lame duck Mayor, who no one was talking to, but John could see that the Mayor was trying to get into the conversation between them, but they weren't having it. The Chief spotted John and told him to join them. John walked over to his boss and shook his hand. The Chief said, "Senator Clayton, this is John Campbell, my lead detective. He's in charge of the investigation, and frankly he's the one who I count on to help me run the department." John trying not to blush was shocked by that statement because John never worked with the Chief until now, but John took the compliment in stride and shook the Senator's hand. "Senator," John said while shaking the hand of the most powerful man in Massachusetts. The Senator replied like the freaking King of Spain, "Nice to meet you Lead Detective. You have one hell of a job to do, and if you need anything, anything at all to help you find the bastards that did this, please don't hesitant to call." The Senator snapped his fingers at his aide who produced a card with the Senator's personal telephone number on it. Giving the card to John, the Senator asked for a photo with John and the Chief, but he asked the Mayor to step aside causing the Mayor to turn crimson red. The Mayor feeling that he wasn't wanted turned abruptly around almost knocking over Mrs. Clayton who was entering the tent.

"God Damnit! You fucking moron watch where you going," screamed Mrs. Clayton. The Mayor's manhood quickly escaped him, and everybody in the tent stopped talking and stared in their direction. The Mayor sheepishly apologized to Mrs. Clayton like a butler who forgot to butter her toast. Knowing that people were watching the Mayor tried to save face, but it was way too late, so he continued to head out of the tent and ran right into the media who'd filmed the whole confrontation.

"MAYOR! MAYOR! HOW DOES IT FEEL TO HAVE YOUR BALLS HANDED TO YOU BY A WOMAN?" The media asked. The Mayor thought that the asshole probably worked for "TMZ." The Mayor and his aides pushed passed the crowded media section and jumped into the backseat of a car. "FUCK! FUCK! WHO DOES THAT BITCH THINK SHE IS? I'M THE FUCKING MAYOR OF BOSTON!" The Mayor's aides failed to stifle the Mayor's tirade; the media caught every word of it as the flunkies finally got all of the windows rolled up. The defeated Mayor thought about killing himself right there on the spot if he had a gun. The car took off leaving the media to go live uncut with a "SPECIAL REPORT." Everyone's cell phones blared billboard top hits as they configured an appropriate way to spin the story and contacted their headhunters. The Mayor knew the Clayton's political connections, and he couldn't imagine a way to recover from the ramifications of his outburst, so he concluded that he might as well go back to his office and start packing.

Back at the sight, Mrs. Clayton ate the spotlight as reporters gathered sound bites. She wave at the crowd, "I love you more than the red carpet." She strolled into the tent and joined the Chief's conversation with her husband. The Senator never the one to be caught off guard introduced his wife to the Chief of Police and John. Mrs. Clayton graciously shook each individual's hand and told them that the Boston Police department had the full support of the Clayton's resources. Senator Clayton, not to be outdone by his eccentric wife, asked for pictures to be taken with his wife, the Chief, and John. They gathered in closely from left to right---the Senator, the Chief, Mrs. Clayton, and John. The photographer was about to take the picture when John felt Mrs. Clayton's hands slithering down his back to his cheeks, and before he could do anything CLICK, the photograph was done. John not knowing what to do thought about what happened to the Mayor and just filed it in his brain as an accident. The Senator and the Chief continued to talk some more leaving Mrs. Clayton and John to converse alone. "So detective do you have any leads yet of who caused this devastation?" Mrs. Clayton said trying to sound genuinely concerned.

John replied, "We have a few leads that we're checking on as we speak ma'am."

"When my husband goes back to Washington in a few days I would like for you to come by my office and talk sometime. You see I'm the chairperson for the Policeman Auxiliary, and I would very much like to get your input on things." Mrs. Clayton said looking hungrily at John.

John blankly looked at Mrs. Clayton and thought, "Is this woman flirting with me in front of her husband? Damn that woman has guts." John graciously declined Mrs. Clayton's offer telling her that since he's the lead on the investigation that his time was limited. Mrs. Clayton refused to take no for an answer, so she reached into her purse, took out her personal business card, put it inside of John's coat pocket, and patted it with an open palm. Then she turned and walked to her husband and the Chief.

Chyna walked up to John smiling. "Ummm, what the hell was that about? I saw everything. Was she flirting with you?"

"She actually touched my ass when we were taking pictures." John laughed.

"Get the fuck out of here! Are you serious?" Chyna nearly exploded with laughter, but she caught herself.

"Yeah and you should've seen how she treated the Mayor a few minutes ago." Chyna told John that she'd already heard about it on the news. John looked at Chyna with a look of surprise, "What do you mean you just heard about it?"

John followed Chyna as she strolled over to the donuts and coffee table. "Yeah it's all over the news, and the cameras even picked up the Mayor's tirade inside his car. Man he went off on Mrs. Clayton."

"Damn." John thought the Mayor was about to get his ass kicked again when Mrs. Clayton finds out about it. Remembering that Mrs. Clayton put something in his coat pocket he reached for it, pulled it out, and looked at the card. Then something clicked inside of his head. John took out the other business card that he got from the evidence bag from their homicide victim, Tara, and noticed that the two cards were the same. "What the fuck?" John said softly to himself. Chyna munching on an apple fritter looked at her partner, "What?" John gave the two business cards to Chyna, and she almost choked. Nervously, Chyna looked over to Mrs. Clayton then to John and said, "Do you really think she had something to with Tara's murder?"

"That is damn peculiar. Why would a socialite, married to a Senator, give her personal business card to a woman who has no money, no power, and not even an elite family name?" John's perplexed glance shook Chyna's core.

Chyna said, "Let's ask her. She's right there." John looked at Chyna as if she'd lost her freaking mind.

"Should I have your ass drug tested? If we walk up to her with our assumptions and question her about her relationship to the victim in front of her husband and the Chief, and she denies it, do you know what will happen?"

Chyna immediately shushed John. "Yea you're right. And no I don't need drug testing asshole."

John looking back at the business cards, turned them over, and noticed that Tara's card had a personal cell number on it. "Let's wait until they leave and talk with the Chief about the best strategy for this situation. I think that Mrs. Clayton is up to some dirty shit." John regarded Mrs. Clayton with great interest. When Mrs. Clayton glanced over her shoulder at John with a come hither look John thought, "That's a cold ass woman."

CHAPTER NINTEEN

The Senator and Mrs. Clayton finally made their exits to their adjacent cars. The Senator answered a few questions from the media, but the main focus was on the belittling of the Mayor by his wife. The Senator not known for dribble drabble excused himself and made his way past the herd to his limo leaving his wife to fend for herself. Mrs. Clayton didn't care. She loved the media---to her the media was like a tampon---you use it for a few days and get rid of it after. Mrs. Clayton told the media that she didn't mean to speak to the Mayor that way, but she was distraught about the devastation of the Police headquarters and all the chaos that occurred in her beautiful city. She told the media that the first chance she got she was going to call the Mayor and apologize for her behavior. She also promised to offer financial assistance to the Mayor's office to help with the budget crisis. With that the media was like a bunch of hungry baby birds with their beaks open waiting for their mother to give them something to eat. Mrs. Clayton waved to the media, entered her car, and drove away with a smirk as big as the Grinch that stole Christmas. "The Mayor is fucked. First he scratched my STUART WEITZMAN'S shoes, and then he curses me on national television. That motherfucker better jump out of that office window or put a bullet through that narrow brain of his. His time in office is about to come to an abrupt end."

John and Chyna approached the Chief and ensured that no one was within earshot of what they were about to say. John told the Chief about what he found on the victim's personal belongings which was the business card with Mrs. Alice Marie Clayton's name on it. "Plus here's the cell phone number printed on the back, and the business card that she slipped into my breast pocket with the same info."

"So what does that have to do with anything?" The Chief demanded.

John answered, "Just an observation, but look at the cards Chief." The Chief took the cards from John and examined them, but he wasn't impressed by their similarity. So he looked at John with a dumbfounded look of, "OKAY."

"What were the initials on the package?" John asked trying to pull the puzzle together for the Chief.

The Chief looked over his make shift desk, found the card, and gave it to John. The card initials were A.M.C. John smirked at his boss and said, "A.M.C., ALICE MARIE CLAYTON!"

The Chief shouted, "SON OF A BITCH! You may have something, but watch your ass John. If you fuck up it's more than your job at stake. If she isn't forthcoming don't push it John. You know who she is and what she is. That woman's piss could distinguish hell fire."

John sensed his boss's reluctance in pursuing Mrs. Clayton. "Boss, did you know when we were taking pictures Mrs. Clayton grabbed my ass." The Chief looked at him and smiled and called him a lucky bastard.

The Chief turned his attention to Chyna and asked what she found at the victim's home. Chyna told them that the home was wiped clean. "Too clean for my liking, but the only thing I found was a piece of scratch paper with a phone number and a reporter's name, a Maria Bradshaw, who works for the National Reporter in South Boston." John asked Chyna if she had called the number, she said yes, but got no answer. The Chief knowing that John wouldn't stop with the Clayton thing told John to go ahead and meet with her but just go fishing and get back to him if something turns out. John agreed to comply with the Chief's instructions. Chyna decided to follow up with Maria Bradshaw about anything she knew about the victim. They both left the tent and headed their separate ways.

While in the car John called Mrs. Clayton's private number and asked for a meeting with the socialite. He expected to hear a tirade like she gave the Mayor, but surprisingly she was eager to speak to him. Mrs. Clayton invited John to her residence in Cambridge in about an hour, and said that she'd be waiting. John thought, "What the hell was that in her tone? Does she think I'm coming over for a mid-afternoon screw?" John thanked Mrs. Clayton and disconnected the call.

Another call came in. It was from Chyna. John answered, "Whatcha' got?"

Chyna said, "I got in contact with that reporter, Maria Bradshaw, and she wants to meet up with me."

"Okay," John said, "When?"

Chyna replied, "Tonight at her place."

John looking perplexed in the rear view mirror asked, "Why her place? Why not in a coffee shop or at the newspaper?"

Chyna said that Maria was working on a big story, and she feared that something may have happened to her informant. Listening, John asked who her informant was, Chyna said, "Tara Meyers…our vic."

"This is becoming some real sticky shit Chyna," John said.

Chyna asked, "I know what you want me to do?" John told Chyna to go ahead and get all the info she could from Maria and to report back to him ASAP. Before hanging up, Chyna asked John if she should tell Maria that

Tara was dead. John said that it was okay for her to tell Maria, but he instructed Chyna receive more information than she gave out any information. They hung up their phones leaving John to his thoughts.

John thought about calling Reese and decided against it; he didn't want to come off all needy, but he made a mental note to text her later to see how she's doing. John made his way to Cambridge to visit Mrs. Clayton at her estate. John noticed that the neighborhood looked familiar. Looking around John started to remember that the Withers' estate was in the same area. John's mind flashed back to Jim and Reese's wedding day. "It was a beautiful day. The food was great, and the bar…what can I say about the bar…150 types of beer, 200 types of vodka and plenty of uppity class women who looked like they hadn't been fucked since "CHEERS" went off the air. GOD DAMNIT!" John screamed out loud. John pulled his car over and called Chyna. Chyna answered, "Yeah what's up"?

John grabbing his note pad said, "What was the name of the catering company Tara worked at?"

"Hold on, let me check." John waited impatiently for Chyna to return. "Got it. It's called "FOREVER MORE CATERING" in Boston the number is (857)555-2359. The manager's name is Greg Peterson. Why you ask…you have something?" There wasn't an answer because John had already hung up after hearing the manager's name. John called the catering service and asked for Greg Peterson, and after about a minute or two Peterson finally got to the phone sounding annoyed,

"Yeah, this is Greg. How can I help you?" John provided Greg with his credentials and asked for information dating back two years. John asked, "Did you cater a wedding for the Withers a couple years back?"

Peterson finally cooperating said, "Let me check...two years...Withers...Withers...ah yes! Withers Party. Yes sir that was our most successful party to date." John cut him off and asked did Tara Meyers work that party; again Peterson put John on hold to check the roster. Peterson came back and said, "Yes, Tara worked that party but got a reprimand for that day."

"Why?" John quickly ejected.

Peterson said Tara disappeared for about an hour and couldn't be found. "I actually caught her coming from the guest house without her tray." John thanked Peterson and hung up.

John suddenly began to feel ill; he remembered that day when he and Jim both got drunk, and when Jim told him that the catering girl kept eyeing him. John remembered that he told Jim to go ahead since he was never going to have sex outside of marriage anymore. Jim told John to watch his back while he took the catering girl up to the guest house and fuck her brains out. John began to laugh as he saw Jim walk up to the girl and watched as he followed his best friend and the girl to the guest house. Thinking more clearly now than he did that day, John continued to remember what transpired between Jim and Tara. John figured if it was that easy for Jim to get laid than he didn't mind sloppy seconds, so he followed them to the guest house and waited for his turn. He remembered going to the bathroom down the hall to take a leak, and when he finished he saw an older woman going into the laundry room then seconds later the Tara ran out sobbing leaving Jim and the older woman in the room alone. John walked up to the door, gently opened it, and saw his partner of 25 years banging the dog shit out of this woman. Discreetly closing the door back, John remembered smiling to himself while walking out to the reception area where he noticed Reese staring at him with a sorrowful, distraught look. John just looked at Reese as she turned and continued to greet her guest. John began to feel like the devil's own piece of shit felt...completely guilty for egging his friend on. He didn't want his best friend to get married, but Jim did it anyway. Afterward

Jim walked over to John and said, "Dude you'll never guess who I just banged up the ass?"

"That cater girl?"

"Yeah, and guess who comes busting in like a fucking cop?"

John, knowing full well that the girl he was screwing left sobbing and another woman took her place asked, "Who?"

"Mrs. Alice Clayton, the Senator's wife! She came in and told the catering girl to get the fuck out and told me that if I don't fuck her she'll tell Reese, so I banged that woman like she was a hobbit at a porn shop." Jim bragged.

John had known Jim for over 25 years; John knew his partner didn't give a shit about other people's feelings, but John still didn't have the heart to tell Jim that Reese might suspect something.

Coming out of his trance John felt remorseful for pushing his friend to have sex with Tara on his wedding day. And now he couldn't erase Reese's image from his mind.

But now John also began to see an intricate connection between people and events. "Everything is starting to come full circle, and it's coming back towards Mrs. Alice Clayton." John called the Chief and explained what happened during Jim's reception, that Mrs. Clayton was there, and how Jim had sex with her in the guest house along with the victim. The Chief couldn't believe what he was hearing from John, "You mean to tell me that Jim screwed the victim and Mrs. Clayton on his wedding day, and that Mrs. Clayton threatened to tell his wife about the affair?"

All John could say was, "Yes Sir."

"Okay," the Chief said, "Do what you have to do to get that bitch talking, but again Lead Detective Campbell tread lightly understand?"

"Lead Detective Campbell? He's never called me that; he only uses my rank when addressing other people." John thought, and then he replied, "Yes, sir." He hung the phone up and began to write on his note pad. John wrote:

ALICE MARIE CLAYTON

1) WITHERS' WEDDING TWO YEARS AGO/THE AFFAIR

2) BUSINESS CARD ON TARA

3) HOW DO YOU KNOW TARA?

4) FAMILY BACKGROUND

5) SENATOR'S COMMITTEES

6) …

John's phone rang, and he picked it up, "Detective Campbell."

It was his friend, a manager at the Four Seasons Hotel, "Come by when you get the chance. I have something very important to show you."

John said, "I'll be over shortly. Thank you." Hanging up, John looked at his note pad and saw that it wasn't much to go on. He had to conceive a more clever way to approach Mrs. Clayton. Since he couldn't concoct a conscientious methodology, he called Mrs. Clayton on her private line and asked to reschedule their meeting because he needed to review new evidence. Mrs. Clayton sounded quite understanding over the phone, and she told John to contact her secretary tomorrow, so that she could fit him into the schedule. John thanked her, put the car into drive, and made a sharp U-turn back to Boston.

Meanwhile, Alice Clayton sat in her office wearing nothing but a sheer satin bathrobe and high heels watching the estate's security monitors with CCTV cameras which the Senator's Security detail had installed a few years back. Mrs. Clayton was looking at John's car as it did a U-turn in the street. Alice didn't like to be stood up; especially by a fucking beat cop. She continued to look at the monitors until John was out of sight.

"Now what," she thought, "Oh yeah, the fucking Mayor." Alice called her new crew to place an order of termination since her other contractor hadn't called her back, but Alice knew that she would have to take care of that loose end too. The leader of the crew answered the phone. Alice told him what needed to be done, when it needed to be done, and she expressed that she wanted it to be messy. The leader confirmed the order, and he told Alice that he would get back with her with the details. Alice still felt aroused despite John's decision not to come over, so she decided to take a cold shower and a nap.

CHAPTER TWENTY

John arrived at the Four Seasons Hotel to meet up with the manager. John parked by the service entrance and got out. He headed towards the service manager's office and knocked twice. John heard, "Come in." So, John entered finding and older man about 70 sitting at a desk. "What in the hell did your old ass call me for? You run out prunes?" John said.

The older man looked up with his glasses teetering on the bridge of his nose and answered with a droll Bostonian accent, "Nawww, your momma brought me some last night for dessert after I had her dinner, smart ass." The two men hugged. "How're you doing nephew?" John laughed at his Uncle Mike, who wasn't really his

Uncle at all, but he knew Mike for a very long time, and Mike was a close family friend, so John resolved to call him Uncle Mike. John sat in one of the empty chairs, exhaled, and said, "Everything is going to hell Uncle. I have this case that's about to topple a major family and send ripples through Boston like you've never seen before." Uncle Mike didn't ask questions about John's cases; he just listened to them and gave his opinion if asked for it.

"I know that you'll handle the situation like you've always have nephew, but that's not the reason why I called you over. I was gone for a few hours early today and discovered something extremely odd. I pulled up and noticed that there was a white utility van parked at the service area door. Now before I left, all the deliveries were done for the day, and I put Bill in charge while I was gone. Anyway," Mike got up, headed to the DVD player, and pressed start, "This is what was caught on video." Mike moved over to let John view the footage. There it was. Five men in white coveralls putting a large rug in the back of the van, but John couldn't tell what, if anything, was inside because it was wrapped in linen and tossed into the back of the van. What truly caught John's eye was Mrs. Alice Clayton talking to them and appearing to exchange a large amount of cash with them. John looked at the monitor then back at Mike. "Go ahead take the disk. Someone already erased the other disk from the recorder, but they didn't get the nanny cam I set up behind the door." John thanked Mike with a pat on the back told him that once everything settled down that they'd go to a Pats game.

John called the Chief and told him that he had cancelled his appointment with Mrs. Clayton, but he had something for the Chief to look at that'd probably put Mrs. Clayton into a compromising position. As John headed toward command post, he thought about Reese and that day, he decided that he'd call her tonight to square things with her. Then John called Chyna to ask her what time she was going over to the reporter's house. Chyna answered, "About 9:00 pm."

"Keep him informed Chyna." Click. John arrived at the Command Tent and ran straight for the Chief, "You got to see this shit." John popped the DVD in the player and pushed play. The Chief stood there watching the images as good as if it was live.

The Chief said, "Where did you get this?"

John answered back, "A source at the Four Seasons."

"Problem is we don't know what's inside that bundle. Yes it's long enough for a body, but whose body and again nothing but conjecture." The Chief replied. "Okay. I'm thinking now that Mrs. Clayton is using my city as her personal playground. I want her questioned first thing tomorrow. The gloves come off as of now. Let me know if anything comes from it."

"Will do," John replied. As John left the tent, he realized that he had not been home to shower or eat.

"Damn," he thought, "all this ripping and running I've been doing. I know I must smell like dog shit. What it's been over 16 hours since I've eaten or taken a shower." So, John went home to get a little "me time" away from all the chaos, but his mind kept floating back to Mrs. Clayton and her involvement in all of the recent major crimes. Everything most certainly pointed towards her, but more importantly was Senator Clayton apart of it also? It didn't matter to John; John knew that after the investigation was complete that someone's ass was going to prison or would wind up dead with a capital fucking D.

9:00 pm. Chyna arrived at Maria's house. Maria invited her in, and they went straight into Maria's kitchen. Maria offered Chyna something to drink, but Chyna declined. Chyna took out her notepad preparing to take notes when Maria was ready. Maria poured herself some tea, sat down, and began. "First of all, Detective Taylor what happened to Tara? I haven't heard from her in a couple of days, and she normally calls or sends me a text message to let me know how she's doing." Chyna tried to figure out the best way to reveal Tara's death. After searching her notepad for a hint of sympathy, Chyna looked up to Maria and gave her the bad news. Chyna told Maria that Tara died from a carjacking incident the other day. "Are you talking about the murder on State Street?" Maria asked. Chyna nodded.

"What can you tell me about the story you're about to put out?" Maria went into the details about Tara being Mrs. Clayton's secret lover, the recordings and photos stashed at her house, and Tara's trailing of Mrs. Clayton's whereabouts over the past week. Chyna mentioned that she'd already investigated Tara's apartment and found the place completely wiped cleaned. Listening intently, Maria knew something was seriously wrong. Maria continued to tell Chyna about the money Mrs. Clayton paid for Tara's services, how they first met at the Withers' wedding a few years back, and that Mrs. Clayton probably hired a hit man to take out an ex-lover.

"I think he was a policeman named…" Maria looked at her many notes and came upon a name that almost knocked Chyna straight to the floor, "a Jim Henry. Tara overheard Mrs. Clayton talk about severing Jim's brakes…enough to cause him to have an accident, but not enough to draw any attention to the brake lines." Chyna couldn't believe what she was hearing.

"This shit is coming straight out of a "DEAN KOONTZ" novel. So, Tara probably died because she was a loose end, and she had evidence---evidence we don't have." The meeting with Maria took a little less than an hour. Chyna thanked Maria and promised to share any info concerning the case with her. Chyna and Maria shook hands; Chyna exited the house, walked down the steps, and got into her parked car. Chyna's head was still swimming after the info Maria gave to her; Chyna started the car and drove away.

Chyna called John and told him everything that Maria revealed to her. John demanded that Chyna return to Maria's house to gather her notes. Chyna, frustrated with doing the grunt work, told John that she would comply with his request. Chyna turned the corner and then another corner when she spotted a muscle car parked near Maria's house, and someone exiting the vehicle carrying a black bag. Chyna quickly pulled over, turned the headlights off, and parked. "Odd," thought Chyna. She continued to sit there watching the outside of Maria's house. Chyna took out her notepad and wrote down everything Maria said about Tara.

CHAPTER TWENTY ONE

9 pm Rita awoke from her sleep, took a shower, got dressed in her secret closet, and armed herself. This time she grabbed a silencer off the wall to use with her Smith and Wesson 500 (the most powerful gun in the world). Afterward, Rita left through the private entrance, took the GTO, and headed for Maria's house. Rita figured it was time for them to meet face to face.

10 pm Rita arrived in Maria's neighborhood and parked her car two blocks down. Rita remembered the way to Maria's house from her previous visit. Rita began to stealthily maneuver through the back yards, avoiding light timers, and barking dogs. She made it to Maria's house without disturbing anything or anyone. Rita noticed that Maria's car was parked in the driveway; with the palm of her hand she touched the hood to check the heat of the engine to determine how long Maria had been home. The engine was warm. Rita figured that Maria had been home about an hour, hour and a half. Rita withdrew a cloth from her pocket and wiped her hand print off the hood. Then Rita focused on the house; there weren't any lights on downstairs, but there was a faint light upstairs. Rita went further to the back of the house where she plotted her entry way into the house. Rita knelt down and opened her tool bag retrieving a window cutter, but her cell phone vibrated. Rita grabbed the phone and saw Alice Clayton's id. Rita realized that she had forgotten to check her messages all day. Rita still didn't bother to check the message though; she'd do it later because she needed to concentrate for the task at hand--dealing with this conniving BITCH and then she'd concentrate on taking care of Clayton's evil ass.

Rita carefully used the cutter on the window pane turning the device with a steady 360 degree turn. After she made the cut, Rita reached into her pocket, grabbed a suction device, and placed in the middle of the circle. Knowing that Maria didn't have a security alarm installed in her home, it was quite easy for Rita to break in. Rita removed the cut piece of glass and placed it in her bag. While peering inside the house to ensure there weren't any surprises, Rita extended her hand through the hole and turned the top lock on the door clockwise until she heard a click. Then Rita pulled her arm out, gathered her things, and entered the house. The door opened with a minor squeak causing Rita to pause for a few seconds to let the noise pass. Sensing that nothing was going to come from it Rita slowly opened the door a little bit more until she could safely pass through without taking a bigger risk in opening the door even more.

    Rita, now standing in Maria's home, surveyed her surroundings, took out her Smith and Wesson 500 (the most powerful handgun in the world), and attached the silencer that was specially made to fit the peace keeper. Rita retrieved a manila folder from her bag and headed upstairs to Maria's bedroom. Rita quietly made her way up the steps and noticed that the faint light she'd noticed outside originated inside Maria's bedroom. Rita, now crouched in a military stance with the cannon pointed outward in front of her with elbows locked and finger on the trigger, reached the bedroom door and stopped. Rita controlled her breathing to a steady flow and placed her ear to the door. Rita heard snoring, so she slowly began to widen the pathway, and like a Tiger stalking its prey, she moved forward. Maria snored like a bag of windpipes with piles of papers all around her. Rita walked over and looked down at the papers. Rita thought that Maria had been a busy little beaver; she had quite a few audio tapes marked "SESSIONS: Dr. Withers," pictures probably from her camera phone, expense reports, and the envelope Rita gave her with the money it. Rita curiously picked up that envelope and found that there was still money in it. Rita thought about counting it but decided against it and put the envelope into her jacket pocket. Continuing her search Rita discovered a picture of herself at the restaurant where she met Denise, the Senator's former personal assistant.

Rita thought, "Damn this woman is good. I never knew I was being tailed." Rita decided to wake the heifer up and have a little talk, but first Rita gathered all the paperwork off Maria's bed quietly and placed them in her tool bag. Rita then took out some duct tape to cover Maria's eyes and mouth and plastic ties to tie her ass up.

Rita, now ready to awaken Sleeping Beauty, walked to Maria's side of the bed, pointed the Smith and Wesson at Maria's forehead, and with the barrel of the gun gently but heavily taped Maria with it. Startled Maria awoke from the knock on the forehead, tried to clear the cob webs from her head, and focus her eyes on the intruder. Frightened Maria said, "Who, Who, are you and what are you doing inside my house?"

Rita, in a voice only the devil could make, said, "YOU MOVE AND I'LL BLOW YOUR BRAINS AND WHAT'S LEFT OF YOUR UPPER TORSO ALL OVER YOUR WALL. TRUST ME. I'LL MAKE SURE THE CORONER PUKES BEFORE HE SCRAPES YOU OFF THE WALL." With that said, Maria was so scared that she passed gas, and Rita chuckled and continued tying up Maria's hands and ankles.

Behind the fake wig, sunglasses, fake nose, and crooked teeth Rita began her interrogation of the receptionist/reporter. Rita grabbed the duct tape and covered Maria's mouth and used another piece to tape her eyes shut but held up on that one. Rita said, "I'm going to ask you a few questions, and if I were you I'd answer them truthfully and without hesitation. Do you understand?

Just nod for YES and shit you know what to do. Let's get started shall we, but before we do if you lie to me the penalty for it…well…I'll leave that up to your imagination."

Maria knew her life was about to come to an end. She started thinking of everything she hadn't accomplished while working at a sleazy newspaper---no husband not even a boyfriend. Maria hadn't spoken to her parents in God knows when, and here she was about to die in her bedroom by a person with a big ass gun who dressed like Phyllis Diller. Rita interrupted Maria's prayers, "Now Maria, you've been a bad girl haven't you?" I've seen your reports on Dr. Withers, and I have your audio tapes from those sessions. My question is why? Why are you investigating Dr. Withers?" Reaching down Rita gently pulled back the tape, so that Maria could speak, but her throat was dry as the Mojave Desert, so when she tried to speak the words barely came out. Rita noticed that there was a glass of water on Maria's night stand. Rita grabbed it, gently lifted Maria's head up, and put the glass of water on her lips. Maria drank heavily causing her to spit some of it out onto Rita.

Rita looked down at her clothes, and said to Maria, "Strike one. Now answer my question."

Maria finding her voice said, "I wasn't investigating Dr. Withers…well not at first, I knew that she'd been going through a lot since the passing of her husband, but a friend of mine in Washington said that her parents were about to be subpoenaed to testify in front of the House Subcommittee for an illegal merger with a company in Germany. I applied for a position working with Dr. Withers, and after my interview she hired me on the spot."

Rita stopped Maria, "Why didn't you tell her that you were a reporter?"

"Because I knew that Dr. Withers didn't know about the subpoenas, and my job was to collect all the information I could before the testimonies to get a jump on the major papers. But it really got interesting when Mrs. Clayton appeared as Dr. Withers' first patient. Mrs. Clayton's husband, Senator Clayton, is the one who is conducting the testimonies."

Rita listened intently and concluded that Maria was telling the truth because Rita had seen the documents in Denise's suite the other night. Maria continued by telling Rita that her boss told her to put listening devices in Dr. Withers' office and to tail anyone and everyone of importance. "How did you know to tail me the other night at the restaurant?" Rita asked. Maria hesitated. "Strike Two."

Maria quickly responded, "I was there on State Street a few days ago and witnessed that murder/carjacking, but I was too far away to get a good look at the victim. So, I slowly moved forward while the idiots fumbled selecting a driver for the small vehicle, and I took down the license plate numbers of the van and even though the sedan didn't have anything to do with the incident I took the plate number on that car also and simply ran the plates which came back to the Withers.

"Shit." Rita thought. "How could I have been so god damn stupid? I didn't even change the damn plates. Fuck. If she knows, who else could've known?" Rita made the decision to…."PFFFFFTTT'" the muffled sound of the Smith and Wesson 500 made contact with Maria's forehead exploding everything backwards leaving just her neck. Maria's body spasmed uncontrollably for a minute and went limp. Rita gathered her things, left the bedroom, and exited the same way she entered the residence. Rita made it back to the car and placed the bag inside the backseat.

Rita initially planned to let Maria live and to use her to expose the documents gathered from Denise, but Maria was too dangerous to Reese; no way Rita was going to let Maria fuck up Reese's life. Looking around the neighborhood Rita took out her cell phone and retrieved the message from Alice Clayton demanding face to face a meeting. "What the fuck! This bitch has got to go." Shaking her head Rita started her car and drove off into the dark without lights, and so did the other car that followed.

Chyna followed a suspicious black car leaving the neighborhood, but she couldn't get a license plate number. She didn't want to turn on her lights to get the plates off the car fearing that whoever she trailed might get spooked. Chyna tried her best to stay back until the brake light of the car illuminated the plate. Tensing up, Chyna backed off even more to give the driver more space. The car turned right and headed east on Elm, and so did Chyna estimating that she was probably a couple of car lengths behind. Chyna sped up a little to at least get a partial plate number and run a check on it later. Chyna actually thought about turning on the BERRIES to ruffle the suspect with a routine traffic stop due to the person driving without lights. The driver in the black car then made a left on Sycamore headed toward the freeway. Chyna knew that John had given her an order to go back to Maria's house to gather the materials, so Chyna was hesitant to go any further. Just then the black car sped off like it was shot from a cannon. Chyna couldn't believe how fast that car accelerated; it must have gone from 30 to 90 in a mere minute. Chyna was still traveling at 30 mph shocked and pissed at the same time because she should've pulled that prick over when she had the chance. Chyna shrugged it off and made a U-turn to head back to Maria's house. She tried calling Maria to let her know that she was on her way back, but she got no answer. Looking at her watch she figured it'd only been about 10 to 20 minutes since she'd left Maria's house and goofed around trailing the car.

Chyna arrived in front of Maria's home, parked the car, walked up to the porch, and rang the doorbell. Chyna waited with her hands in her pocket thinking about that car and how in the hell it accelerated that fucking fast. Chyna rang the bell again; still no answer. "That's strange." Chyna rang the bell again and called Maria on her cell phone. Hearing the phone inside the house Chyna got off the porch and looked towards the second floor. There was a light on. So again Chyna rang the bell, again no answer. Chyna became worried and walked to the side of the house past Maria's parked car and to the back of the house. Walking up the back steps, Chyna noticed that there where a hole in one of the window panes. Chyna reached for her gun and pulled it out. She took out her cell phone as she backed away from the door and called John. Chyna softly said, "Get your ass over to 7546 Timber Lane. Someone broke into Maria's home."

John sounding drowsy from his power nap asked, "What going on, a break in? Didn't you just leave there?" Chyna sounding more frantic told John about the car she followed, how it probably spotted her, and took off towards the freeway. As John listened, he hurriedly put on a fresh pair of pants, shirt, and socks and told Chyna not to go in the house without back up. "Call it in and wait." Chyna hung the phone up and called dispatched, which was now filtering calls through a smaller police station.

Chyna went back to her car, opened the trunk, grabbed her vest, and a 12 gauge shotgun. In the distant Chyna could hear the sirens approaching; she stayed near the end of the driveway and waited for the rest of the cars to get there.

John rushed to his car, turned on the sirens, and headed for the address Chyna sent to him. It turned out to only be 10 minutes from where he lived. John heard the heightened chatter on the radio of officers already on the scene which prompted him to pick up the mike and instruct everyone, "Do not approach! Again this is Lead Detective Campbell telling all available cars on scene do not approach until I get there, copy that?" In unison the officers on the scene copied that order. John was approaching the corner too fast; he pushed hard on the brakes making the car screech to a halt. John got out of the car, opened the trunk to retrieve his vest, and joined what looked like the whole freakin' police force. John went under the yellow tape. In the short time it took John to arrive, the neighbors were gathering around gossiping about what could've happened.

John found Chyna, and they both headed for the back of the house. Since there was a hole in the window they didn't need a court order to enter the premise. John reached his arm inside the hole to unlock the door. Upon hearing a click, John gradually turned the doorknob and opened it. Chyna sarcastically said to John, "It's kind of late to be quiet now don't you think?"

John glared at his partner and responded, "Now who's being a smartass. Cover my rear." Tactical went in first to clear the downstairs followed by John, Chyna, and the rest of the squad. The tactical squad leader said, "Downstairs Clear," which was called back to John in unison. Tactical then headed upstairs searching the bathroom, then the guest bedroom, and finally, "AW SHIT! JOHN GET UP HERE!" John and Chyna ran past everybody. The tactical team with their guns pointed towards the floor made a hole for John. John got to the door where the tactical leader was standing. The tactical leader said, "John, it's bad in there," then he moved out the way for John. Knowing that Chyna was approaching quickly from behind, John tried to catch her from looking into the room, but it was too late. Chyna rushed past John and immediately reeled back as if someone hit her in the stomach with hammer.

The room looked like a scene from V.C. Andrew's "The Flowers in the Attic," but the only difference with that was the headless body that was laying on the bed, and the massive brain mattered that was spewed all over the back wall. John couldn't believe the shit that was going on in his city---first the killing of Tara Meyers, the bombing of the Police Station, Mrs. Clayton's involvement with the so called body at the Four Seasons, now this. John looked at Chyna and asked if she could handle this. Nodding her head, she acknowledged that she could. Chyna thought about the black car that she followed, "Could that perp be responsible for this?" John ordered Chyna to find the materials Maria had on Tara and Mrs. Clayton and to wait for him outside. Chyna turned and headed downstairs to the kitchen to begin looking for the Maria's papers and notepads of info.

John, not wanting to compromise the scene or get close to the body until the M.E. completed his work, put on some plastic booties and plastic gloves. Dr. Kim arrived and was startled by the mess that was left behind. He looked at John, and John just shrugged his shoulders telling Kim, "We know the cause of death. Give us a time and weapon."

Normally Dr. Kim would say something off the wall, but he didn't today. He went straight to work. Kim went to the body, took out his thermometer, and inserted it into the victim's stomach. "This woman died no less than an hour and a half ago. She's still warm."

John called the Chief to give him an update. After that he called Chyna on her cell and asked if she'd found anything yet. Chyna said that she looked all over the place---the kitchen where they sat, the living room, the cabinets, everywhere---and not one piece of paper regarding Mrs. Clayton or Tara was present. John told Chyna to make sure that the CSI team examined fragments from the window pane and surrounding areas. Chyna hung up the phone and did what she was ordered to do.

John walked over to Kim and asked, "This had to be a powerful ass weapon to blow her whole fucking head. Can you tell what caliber?"

Kim reviewed the wounds and replied, "If I knew any better someone brought a big ass cannon up the stairs and blow it off." Kim laughed and continued, "The shot was up close and personal. I'll be able to tell you more after I get her on my table. Wait a minute…aw yes…" reaching for some tweezers out of his bag, Kim was admired the blood splats on the wall. He placed his tweezers in the bloody mess, dug into the wall, and pulled out a bullet fragment which was almost intact. Kim held it to the light for everyone to see, "Here is the bullet that spelled the end for our vic."

"God damn! That's a big ass bullet!" One of the officers said out loud.

John turning to everyone in the room said, "Listen up! If you're not essential personal, please leave the room NOW!"

"C'mon! C'mon let's go all of you." The officers and the tactical unit began to clear out leaving the CSI and the ME to do their job.

John took one more look at the victim and felt sorry for the woman; John thought about various ways to die, but whoever thought about getting their head blown off while in their P.J's. He turned to walk out the room when he noticed a schedule on the dresser. John picked it up and read it; it was a work schedule for Dr. Monica Withers. John was about to lose his mind. "What the fuck is going here," he thought to himself. John took the schedule, folded it, and shoved it into his pocket before anyone else saw it. John certainly had a reason to stop procrastinating and to call Reese now. John talked to Kim one more time requesting an update as soon as Kim completed an autopsy. Kim, scraping some of the blood and brain matter off the wall and into a tube, nodded without looking back at John. John knowing that the scene was secure headed downstairs to meet up with Chyna. Chyna still looking distraught warned, "John, I'm not cut out for this. I left New York to get away from all the killing and the mutilations. Shit I can't handle this." John knew exactly how Chyna felt; he'd been sick of it since Jim's death. But what motivated John, day after day, was to see the bastards who committed the crimes pay for it. John put his hand on Chyna's shoulder, "Chyna go home and get some rest, and I don't want to see you until I call you. Go home love. That's an order." Chyna didn't have it in her to argue; she gathered her things, checked out with the log officer, and went home.

John stood on the porch and watched Chyna leave; he wished that he could go home too, but he couldn't he had to make some phone calls pretty soon, and by looking at the sky it was almost sunrise. John went back into the house to continue his investigation while contemplating what time he should call Reese to ask her about Maria.

An officer offered John a cup of Duncan Donuts' coffee and a cheese Danish; he nodded at the officer with genuine gratitude. John sipped the coffee feeling the warm nectar slowly slid down his throat like a boa constrictor swallowing its prey waiting for the hot warmth of god's nectar to touch his stomach. Feeling anew John went back to work.

CHAPTER TWENTY-TWO

Rita parked the car in the garage and put the keys back into the storage box. She grabbed her things, the materials she stole from Maria's place, and headed towards the private entrance into her room. "It's almost sunrise," Rita thought that for these past couple days she'd been pushing the envelope trying to get back on time. Rita was tired---dead tired---and she knew that once she hit the pillow Reese would wake up refreshed and ready for a full day. Rita had the power to make Reese do whatever ever she asked like forgetting certain things and to wake feeling refreshed as if Reese slept for 8 hours. The only rest Rita would get was to try to slumber while Reese was awake, and if, only if Reese wasn't in danger, Rita would get a good day's sleep.

5:30 am displayed on the night stand. In another five minutes the alarm would go off waking Reese up whether Rita wanted her to or not. Rita rushed to undress and put away her weapons hoping she didn't forget anything. She put on her night gown and 5…4….3…Rita jumped into the air with her arms outstretched…. 2…landed on the bed and….1… closed her eyes.

BEEP, BEEP, BEEP, BEEP! The alarm went off without mercy waking Reese up. Reese rose from her bed smacking her dry mouth while stretching her arms in the air. She hung her legs over the edge of the bed and looked at the clock on the stand. Reese reached over to turn the clock off and got out of bed. She strolled into the bathroom and turned the shower on. While the water warmed, Reese went to the vanity and began to take down hair to wash it. Reese paused while looking in the mirror; she thought to herself, "Didn't I have my hair down last night before I went to bed? Huh," she stated perplexed. Reese got into the shower and felt relieved like she needed a shower after a long day of strenuous work.

After taking the shower, Reese went to her closet and selected an outfit to wear. She placed the outfit on the bed admiring her selection. Then she walked over to the television to catch the Morning News. On the screen the Mayor yelled and cursed; well it appeared that he was cursing because every other word was bleeped out. Reese attentively listened to the report, "That's right Mike. It took all of us by surprise." The reporter touched his ear piece trying to hear from the studio.

The camera cut back to the anchorman in the studio who flashed his pearly white caps. "How did all this transpire Cole? What set Mrs. Clayton off…to the point that she'd berate the Mayor in such a manner?"

Cole now looking back into the camera said, "The Mayor was backing out of the tent when he accidently stepped on Mrs. Alice Clayton's feet as she was entered. We have a clip of Mrs. Clayton chastising the Mayor." The studio cut away from Cole, the reporter, to the scene when Clayton tore the Mayor a new asshole on National television. After the clip they went back to Cole, and he continued his story. "As you can see, Mrs. Clayton's shocking reaction resulted in the tirade from the Mayor after he entered his vehicle. And so far, there hasn't been any word from the Mayor's office and after numerous attempts to contact the Mayor well we just have to wait and see. This is Cole Brubaker live from outside the Mayor's office. Channel 5 News Day Break." With that Reese turned down the volume on her television and shook her head questioning whether she should call the Mayor and ask him if was in need of her services. Reese walked back to her clothes smiling.

Reese dressed and had a lite breakfast. She gathered her things, put them in her brief case, and headed out. Charley was in the front with her car waiting on her. "Good Morning, Doc." Charley always called Reese "Doc" ever since she was a little girl.

"Good morning Chuck. How was your evening?"

"Fine. Fine. I was up late last night watching David Letterman and Jon Stuart talk about our Mayor. I never laughed so hard in my life." Charley took Reese's bags and put them in the passenger seat when a manila file spewed out its contents on the ground causing Charley to hustle to gather them. Reese looking at the papers on the ground asked Charley, "Let me see that file Charles." Charley handed the papers to Reese, and she begun to read them. Reese's face turned to ash.

Charley looking at his boss asked, "Doc, are you okay?" Not hearing Charley she continued to read one page then another and another. Looking up from the pages Reese knew something wasn't right with all this. Reese's thoughts ran rapid. "Maria was a spy for a Newspaper. Mrs. Clayton forced her husband's office to subpoena my father to appear in front of a House Sub Committee Hearing for improper business dealings." Speechless and not knowing what to do, Reese got into her car leaving Charley in the driveway.

Reese tried to read while she drove to her office; she knew it was wrong to do both, but this information was outrageous. "How in the hell did Maria get all this information on me and my family? What does Mrs. Clayton have to do with all this and why is she coming after my father this way? So many why's and no answers, but the main thing is HOW DID THIS FILE ARRIVE IN MY POSSESSION?" Reese knew she didn't have it last night, so she wondered where it came from and what she was going to do about it. Reese put down the papers and concentrated on driving. She made it the John Hancock

Building, parked in her parking space, and took everything with her upstairs to her office. Reese looked at her watch and noticed that it was almost time for Maria to arrive. "Good," Reese thought Maria has a lot of explaining to do.

Reese shut all the alarms off and headed towards her office by-passing the kitchen for coffee. Reese felt that she didn't need coffee because she was way too amped for the day. Reese opened the door and put her things down on the desk. From there she walked to the closet door and reached for the listening device that was described in the report. "There was another one," Reese thought trying to remember the location of the other device. "The file cabinet…there it is," Reese exclaimed reaching behind the cabinet. Reese found what she was looking for and placed the devices on the desk. Looking at the devices and the report, she slumped in her chair and began to read more.

Reese was so engrossed in the discovery that she lost track of the time. "10:45 a.m. where is Maria?" Reese called her cell phone, but it went straight to voice mail. Reese left a message. Then, Reese called Maria's home. "Hello?" Someone on the other line picked up. "Yes, this is Dr. Monica Withers is Maria available?" The person on the other line told Reese to hold on. A strange feeling crept into Reese almost the same feeling she had a few days ago.

Someone came to the phone, "This is Lead Detective John Campbell of the Boston Police department. Who's calling?"

Reese was about to throw up, but she gulped and said, "John, it's me Reese."

John feeling exhausted said, "Reese, I was just about to call you."

Reese opened her desk drawer looking for something to calm her stomach, plus she felt a migraine coming on, "John, what happened to Maria?"

"First, did Maria work for you? If so when did she start and what do you know about her?" John sounded differently than before.

Reese tried to answer all his questions the best way she could. Then she asked again, "What happened to Maria, John?"

John knew he had to tell her. "Reese, Maria was murdered last night. Shot dead in her home while she slept." Reese felt the bile creeping up her throat. She dropped the phone and hurried into the restroom to throw up in the toilet. John held on the line heard the retched sound coming from Reese, but he stayed on the phone to make sure that Reese was alright.

Reese, after puking out a lung, washed herself up and went back into the office. Looking down at the floor she found the cordless phone still connected to John. "Hello? John, are you there?" Reese asked hoping that he hung the phone up.

"Yes, I'm here. Are you okay? Would you like for me to bring you something to calm your stomach?" Reese assured John that she was ok and suggested that he call her back later. John reluctantly agreed but offered again to bring something for Reese and again Reese turned him down. Reese had to figure out how she came upon Maria's documents in the first place, and come to terms with Maria's death. "Wow," is all Reese could say. Her head was pounding; Reese got up from her desk walked to the front lobby, locked the doors, and shut the lights off. She went back into her office and into the bathroom to take some medication.

When Reese returned to her desk she noticed a blinking flag on the computer screen indicating that she had an internal message. Reese clicked on the linked, and it asked, "DO YOU WANT TO BACK UP AUDIO/VIDEO DOCUMENTS?" The green cursor continued to flash awaiting its master's answer. Reese pushed "no." The computer asked, "WOULD YOU LIKE TO DELETE LAST AUDIO/VIDEO?" Again the green cursor waited. Reese typed "NO," and the computer asked, "WOULD YOU LIKE TO REVIEW PAST EVENTS?" Reese looking at the screen typed "Yes." "PLEASE SELECT THE TIME AND DATE YOU'D LIKE TO REVIEW." Reese pushed all and automatically every single video and audio were split into 8 different frames on the screen showing movements from Maria in the lobby, making copies, talking on the cell phone, and the "CUE DE GRUA" Maria planting the listening devices in Reese's office. There were also recorded conversations she had with her editor from the paper, and a conversation Maria had while picking up Reese's prescription. Jesus, all this was going on right underneath her nose. Reese continued to watch the computer screen, and something caught her attention. Reese saw herself go into the closet and minutes later come out dressed in something totally different. The video showed Reese wearing a wig, dark clothing, and "what is that I'm carrying, is that a…" Reese tried to zoom in closer on the image. "Where in the hell did I get a GUN?" Reese rose from her desk and went straight to the closet. She turned the lights on and went in. There were some clothes hanging up—like two pairs of slacks, a pair of boots, and a jacket. No wig and especially no gun could be found. Reese stood there with her hands on her hips looking at her closet. "There has to be something here because the video doesn't lie." Reese emptied the closet's contents then walked toward the window to catch her breath.

Then Reese went back inside the closet feeling everything from the carpeted floor to the panel on the wall. "What a minute! That's a secret panel like the one I installed for the security system in the lobby." Reese ran her hands against each panel on the wall until….DINCK, the panel opened revealing Reese's worst nightmare.

CHAPTER TWENTY-THREE

Reese couldn't believe what she found. "How in the hell did I get all this stuff." She thought. Reese inventoried the items that were in the secret compartment. There were clothes, about 5 wigs, money--LOTS of money---and guns----HUGE guns---at least five of them with a dozen boxes of ammo. Reese's mind felt like Neo from the "MATRIX" when Morpheus told Neo to take either the blue pill and forget everything he'd seen or to take the red pill and reveal the true meaning of the Matrix. Reese thought that the whole ordeal was someone's practical joke. She left the closet and returned to her desk looking at the documents that were in front of her. Then she glanced back at the closet that sent her to "Narnia." She debated the idea of calling John to tell him what she found, but she thought against it because she couldn't explain having all those documents in her possession which came from a dead woman or the small artillery that could put a small drug infested neighborhood out of business. "What to do? What to do?" Reese thought, and she had a silly notion. "Rita? Rita, are you there?" Now she was feeling silly talking to herself, knowing damn well that there wasn't a Rita. Again she called out Rita's name. "Rita, are you there? Answer me you sick son of bitch. Okay that's it." Reese thought, "It's time to check myself into a retreat for a nice long rest."

"What the fuck are you calling me for? Shit, I just went to sleep." Rita said angrily. "Damn," Reese thought. "I am insane."

Rita said, "I told you before that you're not insane, but do you listen to ME nnnnoooooo." Reese walked over to the closet mirror to look Rita in the eye. "Well, what do you want Reese? I was trying to sleep. I had a busy night." Rita asked again, but her patience was growing thin with Reese.

Reese asked, "What do you mean that you had a busy night? What did you do?"

Rita didn't like answering questions, but she played along. "Well I had a date, and I got in late. That's all I have to say about it."

Reese feeling like she was losing control over reality shouted, "Did you have something to do with

Maria's murder? And how in the hell did I come in possession of those documents that's on my desk? The documents mention things about my patient, Mrs. Clayton, my Father's business affairs, and my secretary. Plus how did you come by acquiring the small arsenal that's inside my closet?"

Rita for the first time was speechless. "Fuck, how could I have been so careless?" Rita looked at Reese and decided to tell her everything. "Hell she won't remember anyway after I clear her mind of this conversation and everything that she's seen." Rita began explaining Mrs. Clayton's purpose for coming to Reese's office pretending to be patient, how Mrs. Clayton screwed Jim at their wedding in the guest house during the reception, and how Rita worked with Mrs. Clayton as a hired hitman to kill people---like Tara Myers, the crew that killed Tara, that traitor Maria who worked for the National Reporter, and Rita revealed the true culprit behind the police building explosion downtown. Rita exposed all of her deeds without displaying any remorse.

Reese couldn't take anymore; she had to lie down because her medication was starting to take effect. Reese muttered to herself, "How, just how, how can you do these things. It's, it's not in my nature to maim and kill. I just…" Reese collapsed on the couch. Rita took control of their body, stood up, looked around the room, started to plan how she would get rid of the evidence, and decided how far back she would erase Reese's memory. Then there was a knock at the front lobby door. Rita ran to the monitor to see who it was, "Arg. It's that prick cop John

Campbell." Rita wasn't going to answer, but since she had been unconscious for a while, she didn't know if Reese invited that asshole over. Rita started to put everything in the top drawer of Reese's desk, rushed into the closet, closed the secret panel, checked her wardrobe in the mirror, and went to open the door for "AGENT 99."

Rita put herself into Reese mode and unlocked the door to let John in who was carrying a brown paper bag that had a delicious aroma emitting from it. Rita cheerfully invited John in but didn't move from the doorway, "Sorry about the wait John. I was in the back doing some work and didn't hear the knock at the door." God she hated being cheerful; she just wanted to pull her Smith and Wesson out and blow this guy's nuts off.

John said, "I'm sorry to bother you, Reese. I know that you weren't feeling well after I told you about the death of your assistant. I just wanted to make sure that you were all right. May I come in?" Realizing they were still in the doorway Rita stepped to the side.

"Sorry, I just haven't been myself these past couple of days," Rita quipped. John made his way to Reese's office and continued to talk.

"That's okay. It's understandable. I mean you've been gone from your practice for a while. I'm shocked that you've came back."

Rita, hoping like hell she didn't leave any incriminating documents on the floor or the desk rushed in behind him. "Yeah, well I'm thinking of giving up the practice for good. Who knows this may be my last day here." Rita sat in her chair and signaled John to take a seat in the patients' chair.

John forgetting the reason why he came in the first place gave the brown paper bag to Rita. "I brought you some clam chowder and cranberry juice from Sam's."

Rita took the bag, opened it, and the smell bombarded her senses. "Thank you. I appreciate it. Tell me John, how did Maria die?" Putting the bag to the side Rita was now concentrating on interrogating John about his knowledge of the killer. John told Rita that there was a lot of blood but no figure prints, no fibers, or anything. John even went as far to tell Rita that his partner actually followed a car leaving the scene headed toward the freeway. Stunned, Rita thought back remembering she was being followed. "John did your partner get a make and model of the vehicle?"

John thought that was a weird question for Reese to ask, but he answered her anyway figuring that Jim's instinct had rubbed off on her. "No, she couldn't get a make or a model of the car. Why would you ask?"

Rita knew that she was pushing the envelope with her intense questioning, so she shrugged her shoulders, "Just asking." John shrugged too, and then he asked Reese when she hired Maria, and if she knew that Maria worked for a tabloid. Rita, with the best of her ability, tried to figure out when Reese hired Maria, and she knew that Reese didn't know Maria worked as a tabloid reporter. "Damn," Rita thought, "I have to get this fucker out of here before I say something stupid." Rita asked, "How about another dinner date, John?" John was surprised because he thought Reese had made it perfectly clear that no dating would occur. John jumped at the chance, agreed to the date, and suggested dinner at the Four Season's tomorrow night. Rita wrote it down and happily agreed to it. John stood up and headed for the door with Rita close behind. John turned toward Rita and hugged her, "I'll see you tomorrow Reese. And I promise that we're going to have a full dinner this time." Rita stared at John envisioning where she would place the bullet, his forehand or his eyes or… "Sure I too, can't wait." Rita closed the door behind him and locked the door while watching John walk toward the elevator doors. Rita suddenly thought of the NELLY song, "IT"S GETTING HOT IN HERE" No shit! Something must be done."

John sat in his car reviewing his notes and decided to call Mrs. Clayton for an appointment. Mrs. Clayton answered her private line with a dry, harsh tone, "Yes?"

John sensing irritation in her tone asked, "Mrs. Clayton? This is Lead Detective John Campbell, I'm calling…"

Mrs. Clayton interrupted, "I know who you are Detective. What do you want?"

John, trying to keep it professional, took a deep breath to compose himself and remembered how Mrs. Clayton tore down the Mayor the other day. "Mrs. Clayton I would like to come over, if your schedule permits to ask you a few questions regarding some private matters." John finished and waited for a response.

Mrs. Clayton replied, "Let me check my schedule." Without a please hold or hold on Mrs. Clayton just put John on hold. Mrs. Clayton sat at her desk looking at her nails and estimating the time she would get back with John. "Asshole canceled our last appointment, now he's asking for another one…Dumbass." Five minutes later Mrs. Clayton came back on the line and told John that she had 30 minutes to spare.

"That will do. I'm on his way over now." Mrs. Clayton hung the phone up before John could say thank you. "God. What a Bitch!" John said out loud as he started his car up and headed towards Cambridge. Meanwhile, Rita arrived at the carport to retrieve one of the cars to make an unexpected visit to a famous Senator.

CHAPTER TWENTY-FOUR

Senator Clayton was doing an interview for one of the local media before he headed back to Washington. The program was comparable to that of "Face the Nation" which appears on Sunday's. The Senator hated doing these interviews; he felt that the news was such crap, and he didn't watch it. "Who gives a flying shit that Demi Moore and that hack Ashton "Punkass" Kutcher are getting divorced? And how does the weather man tell that rain is on the way, but won't tell you until 10 or 11 at night? Dumb shit!" The Senator actually thought about introducing a reform to congress to change what's on television. "And what the fuck is a "SNOOKI" or a "KARDASIAN?" He asked his aides once to find out who or what they were. As the Senator continued his interview,

Rita snuck into an office, found an employee's badge, pinned it to her jacket pocket, and walked right into the live taping. Rita found a clipboard and picked it up, so she could blend in with the rest of the crew. She stood by a cameraman while he was shooting and moved when he moved. Rita thought that it would be easy to kill the Senator despite his bodyguards who were spread out all over the place. Rita knew that if it was easy to get into a television studio with one of the most powerful men in the country doing an interview that it would be equally easy to assassinate the Senator.

Rita waited until the Senator finished the interview then she casually walked up to him and whispered something into his ear causing the Senator to blush. The Senator nodded at Rita and called his driver/bodyguard over. The Senator did his normal acknowledgements, shook hands with the television crew, and tried to make his way to through the crowd with his driver/bodyguard and Rita. Once through the Senator asked Rita if she'd like to join him at his suite. Rita acted bashful, but she agreed, and they both got into the Senator's limo. The Senator couldn't wait until the door closed, so he could claw at Rita's clothes. His hands went up her skirt, caressed her thighs, and tried to get to her sweet spot. Rita tightened her thighs locking the Senator's hand in between them. Rita said, "How about I do you Senator?" The Senator acted like a little boy in a candy shop, quickly lay back while Rita undid his belt buckle, then his zipper. The driver/ bodyguard looking in the rear view mirror watching his boss get served couldn't help but feel aroused. Hell his boss got all the fucking women. The Senator opened his eyes and gave his employee a smile then closed the partition, so his driver could concentrate on his driving.

About ten minutes later they arrived at the back of the Four Seasons Hotel's service entrance. The driver/bodyguard parked the car and got out to retrieve his boss and Rita. Partially dressed with his shirt hanging out, the Senator exited the limo and instructed the driver to wait downstairs in the car until he and Rita returned. The driver didn't like leaving his boss without protection, but he did as he was told. Yet, he kept a curious eye on Rita; for some reason, his gut warned that she'd be trouble.

Rita and the Senator went up to the Presidential Suite. When they arrived, the Senator opened the door for

Rita and slapped her ass as she walked passed him. Rita was fed up playing the game. She wanted to plan her attack better, but the window of handling this shit was closing fast. The Senator offered Rita something to drink, but she declined. The Senator said, "You are so lovely my dear. I would love to make love to you."

Rita thought, "Get the fuck out here! Are you kidding me? You couldn't come up with a better line than that?" But instead blurting out her bold thoughts, she coolly stated, "Baby you say the sweetest things." The only thing that was going through Rita's head was, "Die, Bitch, Die." Rita couldn't believe that the Senator took her to the same room where Denise invited her the other night, and that made Rita ponder Denise's demise. "Oh well," she thought, "I'll find out later."

The Senator guided Rita into the master bedroom where he began to disrobe. Following his lead Rita did the same but reached into her pocket, grabbed a syringe, and carefully palmed it, so it wouldn't break. Rita went over to the bed, drew the comforter back with one hand, and placed the syringe under the pillow with the other hand. Next, the Senator walked over to the bed and got in. He patted the other side for her to get in as well, so Rita slid in next to him.

Meanwhile, John arrived at Mrs. Clayton's estate. As John approached the front door that resembled the gate to "DANTES INFERNO," he thought to himself, "What the fuck does a person need with a door this god damn tall? Fucking rich people!" Then he received a phone call from his Uncle Mike at the Four Seasons. Uncle Mike told

John that the Senator pulled up with a mysterious woman and was in his private suite. John asked Mike to keep him informed. Disconnecting the call John felt for his notepad and rang the doorbell. He half expected to see "LURCH" from the "ADDAMS FAMILY" open the door with his famous trademark, "YOU RANG…" but instead it was a young guy, maybe in his mid or late 20's dressed in very tasteful suit. "Welcome Detective Campbell. Lady Clayton is waiting for you in the breakfast nook. Please if you care to follow me?"

"Lady Clayton? Breakfast nook? Please if you care to follow me? I know his parents must be really proud." John thought with a smirk.

John followed the young BENSON through the most massive foray he had ever seen. John could imagine putting at least three NBA regulation basketball courts in this section alone. That wasn't all he admired; the living room itself looked to hold a concert-sized audience. John was almost scared to walk on the carpet, afraid that he might track dirt from his shoes. Young BENSON turned to John as they approached the outside and said, "Detective, may I introduce you to Lady Clayton." Mrs. Clayton didn't bother getting up; all she did was stick her arm out like she was the freakin' Queen of England and waited for John to kiss her hand. John figured that he'd play along with the nut job. John reached for Clayton's hand and planted a small kiss. "Mrs. Clayton," John said and continued, "Again, please accept my deepest apology for missing yesterday's appointment. It couldn't be helped."

Mrs. Clayton's face revealed a sign of "I don't give a shit." She asked John to sit and offered him breakfast or something to drink. John politely declined and pulled out his notepad. John asked permission to begin the interview. Mrs. Clayton reluctantly agreed. John began by saying, "Mrs. Clayton, the questions I'm going to ask you are of a serious nature, and if you feel uncomfortable please let me know, and I'll stop." Mrs. Clayton looked out the window at the hundreds of acres of green well-manicured lawn that could comfortably hold at least three Boeing 757s and a fleet of Southwest planes, gave no response. So John started, "Mrs. Clayton, do you know a woman named Tara Meyers?"

That question caught Alice by surprise. Mrs. Clayton said, "No, why should I?" John wrote down her answer on his note pad.

John said, "No ma'am," and continued, "Also your initials are A.M.C. for Alice Mary Clayton?"

Mrs. Clayton started showing signs of frustration with the questioning and annoyingly responded, "YES! What is this all about Detective?"

John knowing that he rattled her said, "In due time Mrs. Clayton. I just have a few more questions to ask." Mrs. Clayton's face became crimson. John asked, "Mrs. Clayton do you remember being at the Four Seasons Hotel a few days ago around say 3 or 4 pm with a group of men?" John waited for an answer; Mrs. Clayton abruptly got out of her seat, pointed her finger towards John, and spewed profanity like the Devil. John pushed the recorder in his top pocket to record her tirade.

"HOW DARE YOU! WHO IN THE FUCK DO YOU THINK YOU ARE COMING INTO MY HOME ACCUSING ME OF DOING SOMETHING ILLEGAL? YOU CAN KISS YOUR FUCKING CAREER GOOD BYE, YOU TOAD HOPPING, CLIT LICK, BOOT SUCKING ASSHOLE!" John just sat there listening and taping everything she said. Mrs. Clayton wasn't done yet though. "WAIT UNTIL I TELL MY HUSBAND THAT YOU ACCUSED ME OF MURDER!"

John popped up and said, "Whoa! I've never excused you of anything especially not of murder Mrs. Clayton. Is there something that you care to share with me?" John knew that Mrs. Clayton had fucked up, so he pushed her even further. He knew that people like Mrs. Clayton felt they lived above the law, and they tended to frown down upon people like him. John pushed forward, "Mrs. Clayton how do you know a Dr. Monica Withers in Boston?"

That did it. Mrs. Clayton went to DEFCON 4, "GET THE FUCK OUT OF MY HOUSE! I SWEAR TO YOU THAT YOUR DAYS ARE NUMBERED ON THIS," before she could finish her threat young BENSON came to her aide asking John to take his leave. Complying with the young BENSON'S wishes, John began to gather his things, but he wanted to ask Mrs. Clayton just one more question to see what kind of reaction he'd get from her. "Mrs. Clayton one more question before I, what was it again?" John looked at young BENSON and smirked, "Ah yeah, take my leave. Did you have anything to do with my partner's, Captain Jim Henry's, death a few years ago?" That statement really caught Mrs. Clayton by surprise. John saw what he was looking for in her reaction. The look on Mrs. Clayton's face said that she did know what happen to his partner. John's anger started to show as well, while walking to the door John turned back and shouted, "AND BY THE WAY! THAT WAS MY PARTNER YOU FUCKED AT THE WITHERS' GUESTHOUSE A FEW YEARS AGO. I SAW YOU WHEN YOU CHASED TARA MEYERS OUT AND HOW YOU FRAMED MY PARTNER INTO SCREWING YOU. YOU BETTER GET AN ATTORNEY MRS. CLAYTON. YOU'RE GOING TO

NEED ONE." John turned away mad as hell. He wanted to arrest her ass on the spot for conspiring to commit murder, but he resisted that temptation.

As John walked through the massive living room, he heard Mrs. Clayton scream, "FUCK YOURSELF DETECTIVE! YOU THINK YOU COULD ARREST ME? GO FOR IT YOU DICKLESS PRICK! I HAVE THE BEST ATTRONEYS MONEY CAN BUY YOU FUCKING HALFWIT! I WILL HAVE YOUR ASS SHOVELING HORSE SHIT WHEN THIS IS OVER."

John, now out the door, got into his car, but he looked back at Mrs. Clayton and sent one more remark, "By the way, Jim said that you were a lousy lay!" John closed the door and quickly started it while Mrs. Clayton bombarded him with insults that'd make a FOOTBALL player blush. John left and automatically called the Chief.

John described the outcome of the meeting and mentioned recording the conversation of Mrs. Clayton implicating herself in Jim's murder and an incident at the Four Seasons. The Chief asked him about his gut feelings about Mrs. Clayton. John told him that she's the type of person, who wouldn't get her hands dirty, but she'd hire someone to do her dirty work for her, and his gut feeling said she was capable. The Chief told John to contact the District Attorney's office to get a warrant for Mrs. Clayton and a subpoena to search her home right away. They ended their conversation, and John placed a call to the DA's office.

John contacted the DA who was named Greg Turner III, a 50 year old man, who was born in Chicopee, just 3 hours west of Boston outside of Springfield. Greg took the call and was quite concerned about the police's findings and especially who he might be bringing charges against. Greg asked John to come in to his office with the evidence, so he could analyze it. John told him that he'd be there as soon as possible, but he needed to follow another lead first. Hanging up the phone, John called Uncle Mike at the Four Seasons. "Uncle Mike?" John said.

"Hey nephew!" Uncle replied.

"The Senator and his companion still at the hotel?" John inquired.

Without hesitation Uncle Mike said, "YEP! Pretty girl too." John told Uncle Mike that he was on his way. But before John could hang up, Mike told him that a young girl was already staying in the Senator's room, and she had never checked out. John asked how he knew. Mike told John that she called down to have someone to pick up her clothing and have it laundered, so the maid did. "But the weird thing is that she never called or returned our calls when we were finished with her clothing." Mike continued, "The maid even went up to the suite to drop the clothing off thinking that she forgot, but the suite was completely empty, no luggage, no clothes, nothing. Then the Senator showed up today with someone." John asked if there were records of that call and if the clothes were still there. Mike said that he had the clothes in his office, and that the owner of the clothes was Denise Richards. John thanked Uncle Mike and told him to keep a vigil for all suspicious activity.

While Uncle Mike was on the phone, he didn't notice the figure listening to his conversation. It was the Senator's driver/bodyguard. After hearing the phone call the driver grabbed his cell phone and called his boss to tell him what he heard, but of course there was no answer. The driver ran toward the elevators to head up to the suite to get his boss.

Meanwhile, in the Presidential Suite the Senator was lying in bed naked with eyes glued to the ceiling. Rita now dressed was looking at him; the coma inducing drug reached the Senator's blood system instantaneously. The Senator's death would be within minutes, and when they discovered his body and performed an autopsy, the report would show cause of death as a very high cholesterol count that stopped his heart. Rita checked the Senator's vitals, and he pulse was getting weaker. Checking the area to make sure that she didn't leave anything behind, Rita heard the Senator's phone hum. She picked it up and saw that he had quite a few messages---the one that caught her eye was from his wife Mrs. Clayton. Rita opened the text and read it. "WHERE ARE YOU!!!? THE FUCKING POLICE CAME BY. I THINK THEY KNOW I HAD SOMETHING TO DO WITH THOSE MURDERS. THEY ASKED ABOUT TARA AND ASKED ABOUT THAT POLICEMAN. WHAT THE FUCK IS HIS NAME THAT DIED A FEW YEARS AGO? PLEASE CALL ME BACK! I'M CALLING THE ATTORNEY."

Rita looked at the message in disbelief, "This stupid ass woman just implicated herself as a co-conspirator to murder." And Rita couldn't be happier since she was the one who actually committed them. Rita looked at other messages on the Senator's phone. One message was from the driver/bodyguard about a minute ago. "SENATOR I'M ON MY UP! POLICE KNOW ABOUT DENISE AND HER DISPOSAL. GET READY ASAP. THE JET IS STANDING BY." A knock came at the door.

CHAPTER TWENTY FIVE

The knock at the door got heavier and heavier resulting in the driver/bodyguard calling out the Senator's name. Rita checked the Senator's pulse, and she could still feel a faint pulse. "Damn!" She thought. "I should've used more." Rita, not seeing a simple exit for a getaway, got ready to do battle with the driver/bodyguard. The door burst open sending splinters everywhere, "Help me! Oh please help me! The Senator is not waking up!" Rita cried out. The driver ran past Rita straight for the Senator; he felt for a pulse and barely got one. The driver looked at Rita like a lion stalking his prey, "WHAT THE FUCK HAPPENED? AND DON'T GIVE

ME ANY SHIT ABOUT HOW FUCKING CAUSED HIM TO BECOME COMATOSE EITHER."

Rita knowing that this was going to be difficult told the driver, 'We were making love, and he just stopped, and he hasn't moved since. That's the truth."

The driver looking at Rita said, "BULLSHIT! WHY ARE YOU FULLY DRESSED? AND WHY DO YOU HAVE THE SENATOR'S PHONE IN YOUR HAND?"

Rita looked down at her hand in disbelief that she still held the phone. Rita thought fast. "I was going to call for help?"

Not believing it, the driver approached Rita, "GIVE ME THE PHONE. NOW!" Rita waited until the driver got closer. The driver repeated his command in a more demanding voice, "GIVE ME THE FUCKING PHONE NOW, OR I'LL TEAR YOUR WHORISH ASS A PART BITCH!!!" That did it. Rita waited for the driver to be face to face with her, and she struck. Rita hit the driver with the palm of her right dead on the bridge of his nose cracking the bone and sending a shock of unbridled pain to the driver's brain. The driver grabbed his nose as blood squirted in all directions, and he tried to regain his posture. But Rita didn't give him a chance. Rita, with cat-like moves, hit the driver with a right hook to the stomach forcing him to buckle to his knees, and then she came with another left hook to the temple. The driver, clearly defeated, tried to get up by studying himself against the drawer with his hands. Rita visualized the last deadly blow—a massive blow to the center of his chest—causing "COMMOTIOCORDIS" meaning agitation of the heart. The impact of the hit caused the driver's heart to stop beating in seconds resulting in instant death. The driver collapsed to his knees and landed face first onto the carpet. Looking down at the driver, Rita couldn't help but to say, "Now that was an ass kicking."

Knowing that her time was limited, she went over to the Senator and felt for a pulse, "I'll be damned. He's still alive. Good I could use him later." Rita picked up the phone, cleaned off any prints, and left it for the police to find. She left the room in a hurry heading for the elevators, but someone was coming up. Rita, looking for the stairs, found the fire exit and ran like hell to it. The doors to the elevator opened, and soon after Rita entered the stairwell, but she waited with the door open and took a peek to see who was coming out. It was Detective Campbell who was in a dead run after seeing the suite's door kicked in.

Rita had to get out of there in a hurry before John called for backup and had the hotel sealed. She ran all the way down to the lobby without stopping and while controlling her breathing. She was so in control of her breathing that she could pass any lie detector test with flying colors. Rita, undetected, went through the lobby doors and out into the public where she hailed a cab. She got in the back seat, told the driver where to go, and he pulled out of the parking lot. Rita looked back to see an array of police cars bombarding the hotel. With a deep breath, Rita finally relaxed.

CHAPTER TWENTY SIX

After the close rescue that saved the Senator's life, John, now in possession of the Senator's cell with the text messages from Mrs. Clayton, felt relieved about the case. John knew he had enough to arrest Mrs. Clayton now. The Chief walked through the crime scene shaking his head, "Damn, how much you think it costs a night to stay here?"

John looked at his boss, "Give me a freakin' raise, and I'll let you know."

The Chief walked over to Senator's driver's dead body. "Damn, now that's what I call an ass kicking." John, now standing by his boss, looked down at the body. "You know who did this?" The Chief asked.

John said, "I think it was the hooker."

The Chief looked at John incredulously, "Get the fuck out here! You're serious? A hooker did this?"

"Probably so. We have an A.P.B. out on her as we speak. She might've gone down the stairwell when I got here." John said.

The Chief looked at his lead detective and told him, "Get Mrs. Clayton. I want her ass in handcuffs but take some back up just in case and make sure you put the Senator's phone in evidence."

John said, "Already taking care of it. And it'll be a pleasure to arrest that BITCH."

By now the media heard that the Senator almost died and reported that he was unconscious when the paramedics arrived at the Four Seasons. The media added that another person was dead, and the name was being withheld until there was further investigation. All the media vans were lined up at the hospital: CNN, FOX NEWS, ABC, NBC, CBS…all the big boys wanted to get a glimpse of the Senator. Mrs. Clayton arrived in her limo ready to put on a show for her public. The limo driver asked if she wanted to go through the back of the hospital, but she told him, "IF YOU DO, I'LL MAKE DAMN SURE THAT I WILL HAVE YOUR BLACK ASS DRIVING FOR GREYHOUND BY WEEKS END."

The driver said, "Yes ma'am, sorry ma'am."

"God damn right you're sorry, sorry good for nothing sack of camel shit." Mrs. Clayton still seethed over the interview with John which left her feeling venomous. She wasn't going to take anymore shit from anybody. The car pulled up near the paparazzi, and after exiting the vehicle and brushing past the media with cameras and microphones to open Mrs. Clayton's door, the driver was asked who was in the car among other questions. The driver didn't stop he continued on to the right passenger side door to let his boss out. The door opened and out stepped Mrs. Clayton with mascara running down her face as if she'd been crying. She dramatically blew her nose, and when the media saw her they squabbled toward her like piglets suckling at her teat. Mrs. Clayton ate it up, and then someone out of the crowd asked, "MRS.CLAYTON! MRS.CLAYTON IS IT TRUE THAT YOU CONSPIRED TO HAVE POLICE CAPTAIN JOHN HENRY AND TARA MEYERS KILLED?" Mrs. Clayton couldn't believe what she was hearing. "MY SOURCE HAS TEXT MESSAGES THAT YOU'VE SENT TO YOUR HUSBAND SAYING THAT YOU'VE HIRED SOMEONE TO KILL THOSE PEOPLE." Another reporter shouted from the crowd.

Mrs. Clayton, feeling panicked, told her driver to open the door, but before he could John stepped out of the crowd of reporters with handcuffs in one hand and a piece of paper in the other. "MRS. ALICE MARIE CLAYTON, YOU ARE UNDER ARREST FOR CONSPRIRING TO COMMIT MURDER, MURDER IN THE FIRST DEGREE, AND FOR BEING A FIRST CLASS BITCH.

You have the right to remain silent. Anything you say can and will be used against you in a court of law. You have the right to speak to an attorney, and to have an attorney present during any questioning. If you cannot afford a lawyer, in which case like you told me you have the best money could buy, one will be provided for you at government's expense. Do you understand these rights I've spoken to you?"

Mrs. Clayton was shocked and bewildered. "I'M INNOCENT! I DIDN'T KILL ANYONE! I DIDN'T! AND I WAS DOING WHAT MY HUSBAND TOLD ME TO."

The media went ape shit over that comment, questions were shouted, and people tried to take her picture. The police took charge by directing the media back to make room, so John could carefully take Mrs. Clayton into custody. It was a mad house; they followed John to his car where he placed Mrs. Clayton in the back seat.

No longer sobbing Mrs. Clayton did a 360 on everybody, "FUCK ALL YOU! YOU FREAKING MAGGOTS. I'LL BE OUT IN TWO HOURS! YOU PIECES OF COW SHIT!" John closed the door, went to the driver's side, got in, and pulled away from the hospital. Cameramen were still trying to get that one good shot of Mrs. Clayton in the back seat, and she gave them one; she stuck her middle finger up in the air to give them one last good picture of her.

CHAPTER TWENTY SEVEN

The Mayor was sitting in his lavish office watching everything transpire on the television. He had all seven television screens on each major network showing different angles of that bitch getting arrested. He especially loved it when she implicated her husband in the murders. "I can't believe that a family with so much influence and money thinks they can do whatever the fuck they want." The Mayor called for his aide to come into his office. The Mayor sat back with his hands behind his head and his feet up on the desk cherishing every single moment of the coverage. A knock came from the door, "Come in." The Mayor announced. The door opened and in stepped a man who couldn't be more than 21-23 years old, wearing an off the rack suit and Rockport's shoes.

James came to work for the Mayor as an intern fresh out of college. James had a unique way of kissing ass. If the Mayor asked James to lick the toilet bowl clean with his tongue, James would leave it sparkling. "Yes, Mr. Mayor?"

"James, I would like for you to call a press conference to address these heinous crimes committed by Mrs. Clayton and her husband, and I want to stand by the District Attorney in whatever kind of justice he sees fit."

"Sir." James whimpered trying to watch what he said around the Mayor since it was him that didn't roll the windows up fast enough while the Mayor went on a tirade in the limo at the bomb scene. "Do you think that it's wise to conduct a news conference so soon after Mrs. Clayton's arrest? Some people might think that you're going after her for what she did to you the other day."

The Mayor looked at his underling with a look of disgust. "I didn't ask for your fucking opinion, and if I did ask for your opinion you still shouldn't give me your opinion. Do what the fuck I say and schedule the god damn news conference. I want to see that bitch in an orange jumpsuit and shackles. And call the Police Chief I want to make sure that evil whore doesn't get any special treatment."

James couldn't stand being talked to like this. "Who in the hell does this moron think he's talking to? Fuck," James thought to himself, "I hate this fucking job." Then he replied, "Yes sir, I'll jump at it right away."

James got up and left the Mayor's office. He looked at the Mayor's secretary, an older woman of about 65. The only thing she said to James was, "I know. Keep your head up. It'll get better." James still didn't feel all that great. James passed by a bank of elevators on his way to his office when one of the elevator doors opened suddenly, and he almost ran into a large man wearing white coveralls. "Excuse me." James said to the burly man thinking the man had the capability to throw James out of the window with one hand.

"That's okay. It was my fault." The burly man said relieving James tension.. "I've should've been watching where I was going. By the way, can you point me to the Mayor's office?"

James, feeling confident that he was no longer in danger, pointed the burly man in the right direction. James didn't notice that the man dragged carpet cleaning equipment behind him.

"Excuse me?" James said. "Are you supposed to clean the Mayor's carpet today?"

"Yes. Is there a problem? It's been on our schedule for weeks, and the Mayor complained about it so much." The burly man said.

"Well, I'm the Mayor's aide, and I didn't see an appointment on the Mayor's docket for carpet cleaning. Let me go check with the Mayor and see what he wants done. Please wait here."

James left the burly man and headed to the Mayor's office. Fearing that it may have been his fault, that he may have forgotten to put it on the Mayor's docket for today and not desiring another tongue lashing from the dickhead, James decided that he was going to lie about the schedule. Besides the Mayor wanted to do the news conference, so it didn't matter anyway because he was going to be out of the office.

Ten minutes passed, and James, looking like a beat up puppy, told the burly man to follow him to the Mayor's office. The burly man picked up his equipment and followed the young aide. The burly man looked at James and started to feel sorry for him. "Look, you don't have to take that shit from him; this job isn't worth taking abuse from a coward like that."

James looking back at the burly man almost had tears in his eyes, "I know. I know. Everybody keeps telling me to find another job, but times are hard out there."

The burly man asked, "How old are 21-23?"

James said, "Actually I'm 25, but everybody thinks I'm younger."

"Well, find yourself another job. Hell quit, and don't come back to this office. Trust me; the Mayor has his own problems to deal with."

James feeling a lot better convinced himself that the burly man and everybody else was right; he didn't need to put up with the Mayor's shit especially since his political career was so fucked up that the Mayor couldn't find a job in the parks department after this election.

James knocked on the door and went into the Mayor's office followed by the burly man and his equipment. The Mayor was still watching the news coverage on television. Then he turned around and asked James how the news conference was coming along. James knowing full well that the he didn't have time to place any calls to the media responded. "I'll get right on that sir."

"What's taking you so long? What's so hard about picking up the fucking telephone and calling people?"

James looked at the burly man and left the Mayor alone with the cleaner.

"How long is this going to take? I'm a busy man, and I can't stand interruptions," the Mayor stated.

The burly getting his equipment together said, "Don't worry Mr. Mayor by the time I get through with your carpet you'll just want to lay down on it and die."

The Mayor, not impressed by the sarcasm, continued to watch the coverage on TV. The burly man plugged up his machinery, and it began to hum forcing the Mayor to increase the television's volume. The burly man walked over to the door, locked it, went back to his machine, opened a secret compartment, and pulled out a Glock G36 sub-compact 45 ACP with a silencer attached to the barrel. The Mayor decided that the noise was too much; he got up from his chair, turned around to get his jacket off the back of his chair, and noticed a big gun pointed at his face. The Mayor literally pissed his pants. "Wha, Wha, What's going on..." Who the fuck you...?" The Mayor was slurring his words at the huge man with the gun.

"Don't try to push the panic button underneath your desk Mr. Mayor because by the time you reach for it you'll already have three bullets taking up residence in your brain."

"What do you want? Money? I have lots of it; it's yours if you want it. But please don't kill me, please oh, lord please don't kill." The Mayor dropped to his knees and prayed for his life.

The burly man looked down at the Mayor without compassion. "Before you die, I just wanted to tell you that this is coming from Mrs. Clayton. She told me to tell you that she really loves those shoes you scratched up."

The Mayor with a puzzled look said, "I'll buy her a new…." just then the burly man put a bullet through the Mayor's right eye sending a pink and white mess out the back of his head. The Mayor fell backwards with one eye remaining open. The burly man walked over and shot the other eye, so that there'd be no open casket for this bastard.

The burly man gathered his things together and left the Mayor's office. The secretary looking up from her computer stopped typing, "Are you done already? That was kind of fast."

The burly looking at the secretary said, "The Mayor told me to get out because I'm preventing him from watching the news coverage, and he asked me to tell you that he wishes not to be disturbed until the news conference. He didn't even let me finish my work."

The secretary put her hand to her mouth to cover it and told the burly man, "He's such a fucking prick; everybody can't wait for him to leave office; he's just a miserable asshole." The burly man looked at the secretary, smiled, and wished her a good day. The burly man headed for one of the open elevator doors, stepped in with his equipment, and thought about his vacation to Geneva courtesy of one Mrs. Alice Clayton.

CHAPTER TWENTY EIGHT

The taxi pulled up about a block away from the television studio where Rita snuck in to meet the Senator. Rita thanked the driver and gave him a nice tip; the tip was for not talking during the ride. She got out and went toward her car making sure that no one was watching her. When Rita felt comfortable about her surroundings she headed for her car. Opening the driver side door Rita got in, put the key inside the ignition, and turned the key. She hesitated to put the car in drive and continued the thoughts she had in the cab about what went down at the Senator's suite. The way she'd killed the bodyguard was some kind of bloodlust. "I mean the guy outweighed me by at least by 200 pounds, and for him to drop the way he did.

Oh my, that sends a chill down my spine just thinking about this newfound urge I have that's waiting to be unleashed on unsuspecting victims." Rita thought that the rage inside her would be used to kill Mrs. Clayton. All Rita needed was a small window of opportunity to get to Clayton and dispose of her execution style.

Rita put the car into drive and remembered that she planned a date with John, and since she didn't plan on going out with him anyway, she decided to text him to cancel the date. She picked up Reese's cell phone. "Sorry John, but I have to cancel our dinner date. I will call you later, love Reese." Rita pushed the send button, stored the phone back in her purse, and turned the radio onto the news channel, "AGAIN, IF YOU'RE JUST TUNING IN THE MAYOR OF BOSTON HAS BEEN MURDERED.

I SAY AGAIN MAYOR BINGHAM HAS BEEN SHOT DEAD IN HIS OFFICE AROUND 3:00 THIS AFTERNOON." Rita turned the volume on the radio down and was left imagining who would have the balls to kill a Mayor inside his own office in the middle of the afternoon? "God damn, Alice Clayton that's who." Rita sped off towards the estate to shower and change clothes; she made a decision not to allow Reese to reappear until her work was finished with Alice Clayton.

The Senator was now conscious and laying up right watching the news conference on the arrest of his wife. Somehow he had to do something with his wife's twisted schemes to commit murder. The Senator was extremely pissed. One of his aides that was staying at the estate was by his side, "Bill, first of all call my attorney and tell him to get his ass here, and I'm assuming that the police have my phone for evidence, so get me another phone with a secure line to Washington. I need to get in contact with my office to head off this scandal, and call Bruce Locke I need to talk to him about getting a divorce from that bitch before she ruins me, and Bill, tell him to get his ass to Boston as of yesterday."

Bill knew the name Bruce Locke. That name struck fear into people who had the displeasure of meeting him. They called him, "THE LIVED," strange because Bruce Locke's expertise was implementing DEATH to those he met, but if you looked in the mirror at the spelling of "LIVED" you'd see Devil spelled backwards, and that's what Bruce Locke was---the DEVIL. Mr. Locke had a reputation of being the meanest son of a bitch who ever walked the face of the earth. When important, wealthy, powerful people needed to dispose of someone important, they didn't just call anyone; they call on "THE LIVED." The man's reputation stretched beyond the human imagination; Bill remembered the time "The Lived" came to Washington to dispose of a sitting Senator from Tennessee. The Senator was known for getting drunk and hiring expensive hookers, but the Tennessee Senator got extremely drunk with one expensive hooker and spoke to her about U.S. defensive strategies in the Gulf War. Mr. Clayton, hearing of Tennessee Senator's betrayal, called in Mr. Bruce Locke aka "The Lived" to educate the other Congressmen about what would happen if they opened their mouths to other people about military strategies .Well the next day the Senator from Tennessee was found hanging outside a hotel window by a telephone cord, butt naked with a "Y" shaped incision from his chest down to his navel, and his intestines spilled on the ground below, and attached to his skin was a note, "HEAR YE, HEAR YE FOR ALL THOSE WHO REPRESENT THE GREAT PEOPLE OF THESE UNITED STATES WHO MISUSE THEIR OFFICES TO LINE THEIR OWN POCKETS YOU WILL ALSO SHARE IN THE COMPANY OF "THE LIVED." SO I HAVE SPOKEN AND SO SHALL IT BE DONE, YOU HAVE BEEN WARNED."

Bill placed the dreadful call to Mr. Locke and relayed Senator Clayton's message, and after that unpleasantness he called the Senator's office to prepare for the onslaught from the media. "It is going to be one of those days," thought Bill as he went back into the Senator's hospital room.

After finishing the brief conversation with the aide, Bruce Locke placed a call to American Airlines to book his flight from Miami to Boston. He hesitated and said, "Fuck it. It's the Senator's money. I'll just book one of those fancy G6 planes, and I'll get there quicker." He called information for the listings of private jets. When he finally booked his flight for Boston that afternoon he knew that he couldn't bring any weapons on board, so he called a friend of his who lived in Roxbury, which wasn't too far from Boston, to let him know that he was coming for a visit. The call was brief because he didn't know if either of their phones were tapped. His friend understood what he meant by "A VISIT" and didn't ask any questions about how long he was staying; he just knew that the weapons he had stored at his home were ready when he needed them.

Looking at his watch, Bruce grabbed his pre-packed bag and headed out the house for the private airport. The flight shouldn't take more than three hours giving him enough time to figure out how to take out Alice Clayton, and by the way the aide was speaking, the Senator wanted her ass taken out by any means necessary. This put a big smile on Bruce's face because he hadn't killed a woman in a long time. And Bruce had encountered the Senator's wife before. He was going to enjoy mutilating her body. Bruce reached the airport and parked his car in the VIP section; a purser came to his car to help him with his bag. Bruce knew that the purser had to take his bag into the terminal, so his bag could be scanned. From there he headed for the tarmac where his private plane awaited him. He walked up the stairs to the plane where beautiful blond women with slim curves and breasts, that'd make a teenager commit suicide, greeted him. "Welcome aboard Mr. Locke." Bruce flashed back to that movie he'd just watched with John Travolta and Nick Cage "FACEOFF." Bruce loved the part when Nick Cage was on the plane getting ready to take off and asked for the flight attendant to come sit on his lap. The flight attendant sits on his lap, and Nick says, "I COULD EAT A PEACH FOR HOURS." Bruce looked at the flight attendant, smiled, thanked her, and dreamt of eating her PEACH for the next three hours.

"Sit where ever you like Mr. Locke, and before we take off, what type of beverage would you like?'

"I'll take a Sam Adams, Love."

"Would you like that in a glass or bottle?"

"Tell you what sweetheart, give me the beer in the bottle, and I'll take you in a glass."

The flight attendant smiled her customary smile as she knew that she would get hit on. "Oh, Mr. Locke," she giggled and proceeded to close the doors and inform the Captain that they were ready for takeoff.

CHAPTER TWENTY NINE

Upon reaching the Police substation, John looked at the text message from Reese canceling their dinner date. He had forgotten all about it. John figured that after all the mess was done with that he was going to see if there were any sparks between them. He looked in the rear view mirror at Mrs. Clayton who sat quietly in the back seat watching the passing scenery of Boston's real neighborhoods. "Wow," John thought to himself. "With all that money and nothing but time on her hands she couldn't find anything to do with her time or money, what a waste."

Mrs. Clayton felt John looking at her and gave him a smile, "May I help you, peasant?" John was about to say something smart to her when he heard the call on the Police band radio about the Mayor being murdered inside of his office.

"What the fuck is going on in my city?" John said aloud.

Mrs. Clayton also hearing the news over the radio laughed and winked at John. "What's the matter dear? Thinking about running for office? I've heard that there's a vacancy available. Do you need my endorsement?" John was losing his patience with her; if it was anybody else John had in his custody, he would've pulled the car over in a vacant parking lot or an alley, went to the back seat, and knocked the shit out them, but he didn't believe in hitting women. Yet, John contemplated allowing Mrs. Clayton to be the exception.

John looking in the rear view mirror at Mrs. Clayton took a shot at asking a question that was bothering him and knowing of her temperament he knew that she would speak her mind. He knew the conversation probably wouldn't hold up in court, but he just had to ask, "Mrs. Clayton, let me ask you something if I may, between you and me?"

Mrs. Clayton stopped giggling and looked at John through the rear view mirror, "You're going to ask if I had something to do with the Mayor's murder and those other murders aren't you?" John nodded his head. "Let me tell you something detective, knowing that what we talk about in this car is going to inadmissible in the court of law since my attorney isn't present. I can honestly tell you that the people who died these past couple of days deserved to die, and did I do it? No, but I do have the power and the will to do whatever I chose to do to make sure that no one gets in my way and those poor miserable bastards are laying in the morgue getting cut up like pigs in the fucking market. And trust me, I won't lose one ounce of sleep over it."

John couldn't believe what he was hearing. "This woman is actually telling me that she had something to do with these murders."

"Looking on your face detective, you know that I didn't pull the trigger, but you suspect that I had these people killed by other means? Well, let me put your mind at ease, or better yet let's talk about your partner, Jim is it? Oh yes, Jim. It's my understanding that his death was quite excruciating…being burnt in that cheap ass car, but like you said at my house, he said that I was a lousy lay.

Except I remember quite the opposite Johnny Boy; he was actually planning to leave his wife and become my BITCH…"

"SHUT THE FUCK UP BITCH!!!" John lost it. He spewed out such hatred for the woman that he pulled the car over, slammed on the brakes, reached for his gun, and pointed at Mrs. Clayton's head. "HE WAS MY BEST FRIEND YOU UNHOLY WHORE. YOU HAD HIM KILLED BECAUSE OF WHAT, SEX? I SHOULD FUCKING PULL THIS TRIGGER AND END YOUR MISERABLE FUCKING LIFE OR BETTER YET DRIVE YOU TO SOUTH BOSTON AND DROP YOUR ASS OFF IN THE SOUTHIE AND LET THEM TAKE CARE OF YOUR ASS."

Mrs. Clayton didn't budge not one inch. She just smirked at John and calmly said, "You're not going to do a god damn thing you cum sucking prick. You're going to take that gun and put it in your fucking mouth and pull the trigger because when I get out of here your ass will be dead. I promise you. If you think your partner died a horrible death, your death my friend will become legendary." John never met someone as evil as this woman. John was so angry that he had tunnel vision; the only thing he could see was her in the backseat. Everything around them was black except her. He saw Jim and all the good times they had. "What are you going to do officer? Excuse me I meant detective. Not a damn thing! Now let's go bitch. My attorney is waiting, and I have a dinner engagement tonight. You're holding me up."

John dazedly looked at Mrs. Clayton, and he blinked, smiled at her and BBBBAAAAAAMMMM.

COMING SOON IN JUNE

Robert Stevens' second novel

"iMAGES ..."

Made in the USA
Coppell, TX
22 July 2025